SHE IS

WOMAN
COURAGEOUS
COMPELLING
and
CAPTIVATING
(AND SOMETIMES OUTRAGEOUS!)

SHE IS

WOMAN
COURAGEOUS
COMPELLING
and
CAPTIVATING
(AND SOMETIMES OUTRAGEOUS!)

A Collection of Short Stories

Lyla Faircloth Ellzey

To order additional copies of this book, contact:
Xlibris Corporation
1-888-795-4274
www.Xlibris.com
Orders@Xlibris.com
122448

CONTENTS

For Mary, who would have made
a perfect Pink Lady.

ACKNOWLEDGEMENT

For a first time author, many of the things we write about are things we know, or have heard about, or stories that have been handed down for generations and each generation has put its own spin on the tale. We retell these stories, tweaking them a bit here and a tad there so that we make them our own. There are other stories, however, that just appear in our imaginations, as if the information input materialized there by an alien opening our sculls and installing it in our brains. I don't think I have any aliens to thank, but I do thank the people I know whose stories morphed into something else entirely as I entered them on the typewritten page.

Whatever the inspiration for the stories that follow in this book, they are my stories, and from my imagination. I'm grateful that a movie, a song, a phrase, a word in passing, or any interesting topic can give me an idea and inspire me to write it down. One such instance is my story "The Pink Ladies," inspired not by the movie, but by a picture I took at a café in Cedar Key, Florida where three Pink Lady jackets were hanging from the backs of three café chairs. Voila! A story was born! It is included here.

FLOWERS AND FOIE GRAS

"**W**HAT DO YOU want to do for Valentine's Day, Polly?" my husband asks.

We are sitting in our screened-in porch, enjoying this pleasant weather we've been blessed with for several days running. Lingering over brunch, we marvel at the huge male Cardinals as they proudly thrust out their breasts, strutting so that all might see their vibrant red coats.

I draw my gaze from the antics of the grey squirrels, who lithely spring from one bird feeder to the next, scattering both bird seed and birds in all directions, and look questioningly at my husband's face.

"Well," I answer, preoccupied with the day that is happening around me, "what do you want to do?"

It is too lazy a morning to have to make decisions. I push the last crumbs of my lemon poppy seed scone around my plate with a tiny butter knife, the last of the lemon curd clinging to it. I pick up the crumbs, gathering them with my thumb and forefinger, and bring them carefully to my mouth, lest

I should lose one in transit. I adore lemon poppy seed scones with lemon curd.

"I thought we might do something different this year."

"Like what?" If we are going to talk on this sun-kissed winter's day about doing anything, then the ball is in his court.

"Instead of going out, I thought we might stay home."

At the look of mutiny on my face, caused undoubtedly by my thinking this meant we would not celebrate Valentine's Day and I wouldn't get flowers or candy, he was quick to ward off my objection with an explanation.

"No, wait. This doesn't mean that we won't have a good, uh – no, I mean *great*, Valentine's Day. We will. We'll just do it differently than we ever have before." Lamely, he finished in a more subdued voice, "That's all I meant."

"Well, okay then. What do you have in mind?"

"Let me start again. Polly, darling, what would you like to have for Valentine's Day?"

"You know it has got to involve flowers. I don't care what kind. I know that you know how much I love fresh flowers. That's why I buy them at the grocery store each week, so we can enjoy fresh flowers in the house in the winter time."

"I know, darling. I know," he soothingly reassures me. "And I assure you there will be flowers. Lots of flowers."

With his words, my day again brightens, the birds begin to dart among the six bird-feeders he has set up in the yard, and the squirrels resume trying to open the tops of these same six bird-feeders, hanging alternately by their back legs while they pry with their front paws, or gripping the edges of the feeders with their front paws while they kick with their back legs at the stubborn tops. One brilliant buck manages to pry open the top of one feeder and is soon ensconced inside, appearing to be almost as surprised at his successful daring-do as we are. The song birds begin to cheerily sing, and I even discover another lemon scone crumb under the little butter knife and lift it to my tongue. All is bliss again.

The week progresses and Valentine's Day hovers over the horizon, just one day away. I look for some sign that he has lived up to his word and has planned something special. I check his sock drawer. No candy or card there. I check his bedside table. Not there, either. When all else fails, go to the obvious place. Nope, no candy, decorated cookies, or other item screaming "I love you" is to be found in the kitchen cabinet. Sigh. I am resigned to just having to wait.

Valentine's afternoon he drives into the driveway, slams the car door, and rather purposefully strides into the house. I peek at him from the safety of the curtain in the front bedroom. He has bags! Was that the tippy-top of some flowers I see just sticking their heads out of the paper bag? Dang! I can't be sure.

"Honey? Where are you, Honey?" he calls as he sets down his bags on the kitchen counter.

I scoot across the hall to our bedroom, drop into the computer chair, and begin to tap-tap on the keys. I can hear his footsteps coming down the hall.

"Oh, hi Sweetie," I say. "I've been in here typing away. What's up?"

He leans down and gives me a slow kiss. I know he can see right through me, but it doesn't matter. These are the games we married couples play.

"Why don't you just stay back here and work on your project for awhile?" he ever-so-casually suggests. "I'll just be out in the kitchen putting some things away." With a big grin spread across his face, he starts to exit the bedroom, and I'll be left to wonder what in the world he'll be doing out there.

So, looking up and batting my clumpy eyelashes at him, I say, "Why sure, Sweetie. You go ahead and do what you want and I'll just finish up here."

Batting had been a bad idea. I now have the Passionate Purple mascara, guaranteed to make you beautiful and your man happy, in my eye. As he leaves the room, I head for the sink to wash it all off and to start on the "getting-me-beautiful" ritual once more.

Curiosity killed the cat, so they say, but I just can't help it. I have to know what he is doing. I give him about ten minutes after washing out my eyes and I then creep up the hall to the kitchen door and peer around the corner. He has his back to me, standing at the counter. He has a whole array of items in front of him, but darn it, I can't see what they are. He is laying them out on one of my large china platters. That means it must be something good to eat, right? I look around for flowers, but they are nowhere in sight. Did he forget? Oh, please, don't let him have forgotten. There'll be hair-pulling for sure if I don't get flowers. And it won't be mine!

I slink back down the hall. In my bathroom, I look at myself in the mirror. My eye is still as red as if someone had exploded red dye in it. I decide right then that I will never be a bank robber. I put some eye-drops in and the redness disappears like it does in television ads. My eye looks so good until I decide to do the full-monty and put the war paint on. I again apply the Passionate Purple mascara and eye shadow. When I am finished it looks pretty classy, if I may say so myself. I even manage to master the "smoky" look that all the models in the magazines are wearing this year. Gazing into the mirror, I say softly, "Look out, Buster. You're in for a wild night!"

I finish my toilette by applying some Forever perfume from China and donning a pair of sexy silk Chinese pajamas with birds and flowers on them. Flowers! I'd almost forgotten. There'd better be flowers!

Opening my desk drawer, I take out the lovely Valentine card I made for him. I used Hallmark's card making software and raided my scrapbook sticker file and had come up with a beauty. It was for his eyes only. The artwork is sexy and red. The impassioned words of love are sexy and red.

The promises I made to him are sexy and my face is red just thinking about actually fulfilling them.

"Hey, Honey, are you ready for dinner?" He sticks his head around the corner of the bedroom door where I've been holed up now for over an hour. "I think we'll eat in the living room."

"Huh?" That doesn't sound like anything romantic to me.

He whistles appreciatively at my sultry make-up and sexy pajamas. Leering and winking at me, as if he has about a pound of beach sand in his eye, he instructs, "Now close your eyes until I tell you that you can open them."

He takes my hand and leads me toward the living room; my other hand I hold behind my back to hide his Valentine card. I'm not ready for him to see it yet. Maybe after a couple of glasses of champagne. Oh, there would be champagne, wouldn't there be? A fresh, new worry. First the flowers, and now the champagne.

He stops and turns me toward the fireplace. I can hear a spitting and hissing like our cat Jody makes when the next door neighbor's dog chases her.

"Okay, open them!" he sings out.

I do. I stare at a warm, roaring fire licking its way heavenward. "Ooh, that's nice, Sweetie," I say in sincere appreciation.

"And that's not all." He turns me around and points me like a compass arrow at the coffee table. It is now transformed into a banquet table filled with a feast. And there, sitting on the end are two vases. One is filled with a rambling array of yellow and white roses. The other is dripping a perfect profusion of pink peonies. "I didn't know which you'd like the best, the roses or the cut flowers, so I got one vase of each." He stands there like a little boy, eagerly waiting for me to say "Good job."

I gasp. I choke. I lose my breath. I take in a big breath of air and can breathe again. "Oh, my goodness, Sweetie, these are the most fabulous flowers I have ever seen! Nothing could have made me happier." I also use most of the complimentary adjectives I have ever learned.

And there's more!" he crows. "Look!" From behind a couch pillow he pulls out a monstrous box of chocolates. At least two pounds worth. And filled with chocolates filled with caramels, peanut butter, nougat, and all the really yummy stuff.

"Oh, I love you!" I whisper. My breath still isn't coming just right.

"And look at this," he coos, indicating the black lacquered sushi table we use as a fancy coffee table, now almost literally splay-legged with its bountiful burden.

Upon the large china platter he has prepared and placed a fan of smoked salmon, a mound of black truffles, a wedge of pate foie gras, a tier of sushi, and a layer of thin slices of an aromatic light yellow cheese. In a small bread basket, he has placed crispy sesame crackers and only slightly thicker slices of a fine French baguette. On another china platter he has arrayed small dishes of cream cheese, diced red onion, and juicy, fat capers to go with the salmon. Beside them sit tiny pots of wasabi paste and pickled ginger for the sushi.

I turn to him wide-eyed. With a huge smile I rave, "This is magnificent! You have completely blown my mind. How did you come up with all this?"

Sheepishly, but earnestly, he answers. "I know how much Valentine's Day means to you so I thought I'd do something different. I was looking at several of your women's magazines and found all kinds of ideas."

Finally I had gotten my money's worth from the dozen magazines I slavishly devote myself to each month. It seems he has gotten more from them than I ever have.

"Here, my love, sit on this pillow and let me serve you a plate."

I ease down onto the pillow and watch, with fascination, him take one of my prized crystal salad plates and fill it with the delectables on the table. First thing is a slice of the bread plied with cream cheese, then salmon with red onions and capers piled atop it. Next is a sesame cracker spread with the black truffles. Only a tiny bit, as the truffles are quite strong in flavor. Next comes another piece of bread with a sizeable hunk of the pate upon it. A California roll from the Sushi tier is added. Last comes a piece of the cheese.

I am salivating as he sets the plate before me on the table. I actually have a place-setting there, complete with red cloth napkin, silver salad fork and one of my small antique butter knives.

Starting to sit down on his pillow, he exclaims, "Darn, I almost forgot!" He changes gears, so to speak, and hurries to the refrigerator. I hope he will return with at least a glass of wine.

Bless his heart, in one hand is a bottle of Dom Perignon champagne and the other sports two fluted Waterford Champagne glasses we had been given as gifts one anniversary several years back. He sets them down with a flourish, says, "I'll be right back," and takes off again. Wow! Champagne. And Dom Perignon, at that! I wonder what he can possibly bring out now.

This time he returns with a plate of strawberries. Meanwhile I sit there with my mouth hanging open. Catching flies, as my mother would've said. I am utterly amazed by this husband of mine.

He opens the champagne bottle, aiming the cork at the merrily burning fire. It goes about two feet and fizzles to the hearth. A small spout of champagne erupts from the bottle and he quickly begins to pour it into my glass. Done with pouring into both of our glasses, he sets the champagne down and waits a moment for the fizz to subside and then plunks a fat strawberry into each of our glasses.

"Cheers, my love," he says, raising his glass in a salute to me. "Happy Valentine's Day."

Finding my voice again, I croak, "Cheers, Sweetheart," all the time shaking my head in wonderment at this marvelous man. "Happy Valentine's Day to you, too!"

We dig in. We eat and eat and enjoy every bite of this enticingly different Valentine's dinner. After we are sated and leaning back against the couch, he puts his arms around me and we snuggle close together while watching the fire flicker and flare.

Easing out from under his arm, I reach down to where I had surreptitiously stowed my Valentine card for him under the coffee table. Retrieving it, I offer it to him with a suggestive smile. "Here, big boy, this is for you."

He opens it and reads it while I watch his face. His smile turns to a gape, his eyebrows rise to his hairline, and he turns to me with an incredulous look on his face that fights with hope and delight and sheer wonder for the winning expression. A combination, sheer delight, wins.

We rocket up from the floor and all but run to the bedroom. Boy, I have promises to keep! This will be a Valentine's Day for the record books.

THE BLUE STEEL SPECIAL

"A CUP OF COFFEE, please," Joe says to the young waiter, who retains but a small bit of his original perkiness of the early evening. He has spent long hours serving coffee, pie, and the blue plate special.

"Yes, sir."

"You want one, Irene?" Joe addresses his companion.

"What?" Irene is deep in a world of her own; her brow furrowed with what might have been taken for concentration, but was, in fact, very deep unease.

"A cup of coffee?"

Just a confused look from Irene is all he gets in return.

"Do you want a cup of coffee, Irene?" he asks again, this time a little more gently. He knows what is on Irene's mind and why she seems so out of it. He is feeling much the same way.

"I guess."

"Okay, two cups of coffee, please," he says to the waiter, the lone staff member in the café at this late hour of the night. "And cream. We'd like cream, too."

"Sure. And there's sugar there in that jar in front of you, if you want that, too."

"Thanks," Joe replies, trying and failing to provide the waiter with a smile.

He looks at Irene, sitting beside him on the bar stool at the café's counter. She can feel the weight of his gaze on her and turns her head so she is looking at him. She raises an eyebrow and then shrugs her shoulders. Joe takes this to mean that, at this point, she has nothing further to say.

The waiter returns with their two cups of steaming black coffee and places a cup in front of each. Tired and bored, he directs to Joe, "What you doing out so late tonight, folks? Been to the theatre? We get lots of people stopping in here after the shows."

Joe is saved from having to answer because the one other patron of the Midnight Bar and Grill chooses that moment to raise high his coffee cup, signaling he is ready for another.

"Gotta go; I'll check back with you in a minute," sighs the waiter, whose name tag reads "Phil."

"We're fine," Joe says, hoping he'll just leave them alone. Talking with someone, other than Irene that is, is the last thing Joe wants to do right now. He badly wants to talk with Irene, however. They've got to make a plan.

"Watch your legs," Joe now says to Irene, with a pointed look at her knees.

Irene rouses her head from her hands long enough to look down at her legs. What is wrong with her legs, she wonders, before seeing what Joe is talking about. Beneath her hastily thrown-on coat, which is now sliding open due to her crossed legs, Irene has on only a black silk negligee. The negligee's band of heavy black lace, sewn so delicately to the black silk, is there for anyone to see. If there had been anyone to see.

"Who's going to see it? The waiter can't, and," she nods her head toward the other man at the counter, "he's not looking. Besides, he can't see it from where he's sitting, anyway."

"Just cover yourself!"

"Okay, Joe. Anything you say."

This is a snide remark, aimed to annoy Joe. And it does. She is annoyed with Joe. He is annoyed with her. He is as annoyed as anyone can be who has just killed his mistress's husband.

"You know, you shoulda been more careful," Joe accuses.

"Hah!" Head thrown back, looking down her nose in scorn, Irene snorts, "Me? *You* should've been more careful. But no, you said you had to see me tonight, even though I told you Charles would be coming home before midnight."

"You sure didn't act like it made any difference to you one way or the other after I got there and got you in bed."

"Don't be coarse, Joe."

"The fact remains, my dear Irene, that your husband is dead."

Tears appear in Irene's eyes as she says, "Yes. I know he's dead. Oh, my God, Joe! I can't believe you actually killed him."

"I wouldn't have done it if he hadn't pulled that pistol on me."

Retrieving some of the lost loyalty to her husband, Irene responds, "Yes, but he had every right to try to shoot you. You were in a most compromising position with his wife."

"If you mean that I was in the middle of giving you the best sex of your life, then I guess you're right."

"Joe, please don't talk like that. You make me feel cheap, like any of the other trash you've been with."

Joe slides his arm around Irene and pulls her to him. God help him, but he did love this woman. "No baby. If you tried, you could never be like any of those other girls. You're special." He emits a short laugh. "I guess you must have been very special to Charles for him to whip that gun out of the bureau drawer and fire at me." He gazes into the distance, looking at nothing, reliving that frightening moment. Almost under his breath, he says, "Damn! He almost hit me. He could have killed me!"

Lowering her face into her hands again, Irene whispers, "But you didn't miss him when you took the gun away and shot him right in the chest."

"I'm just a better shot. Besides, I was fighting for my life. Yours too, most likely."

"Joe, what are we going to do?"

"I guess we could go back and get his body and take it out of the city and bury it somewhere." Joe furrows his brow and narrows his eyes while he thinks.

"No!" Irene bursts out, raising her voice. Phil, the waiter, looks over at them from his stance in front of the other customer.

"Hold it down," Joe cautions. Phil goes back to listening to the old man drone on.

"No. I mean it, Joe. We're not going to do that. Even if we cleaned up the bedroom, somebody would find the evidence they need to put us on trial for murder."

"Well, I ain't doin' no time for murder; I'll tell you that right now."

"I don't think you'll have to go to prison, Joe. I've been thinking. I think we should go to the police station right now and just tell them the truth. Tell them that we love each other and it just happened. Us being in bed, I mean. And then Charles found us and grabbed the gun to shoot you. And you were fighting for your life when you shot him."

"Have you gone nuts, lady?" Joe looks at her as if, indeed, she has lost her mind.

"Just think about it, Joe. We tell them just how it happened. We have to admit to being in bed together." She stopped and hung her head, a tear slipping silently along the curve of her cheek.

Joe sits straighter, leans back and looks at her as if appraising something offered for sale. "Go on."

"It won't make much difference for you, but my reputation will be ruined. All my friends will find out I've been sleeping with someone, having an affair behind my husband's back. And when they find out it's you, and not someone from our social circle, I'll be completely ostracized." She sniffs delicately and wipes away her tears with a napkin from the counter.

Deciding not to be offended, Joe asks, "But you *do* think they won't prosecute me for murder if we tell them the truth?"

"I really don't think they will. After all, I am publicly ruining myself by admitting to being in bed with you, so I think they'll realize Charles had to have shot first when he found us together. And just look at me. They'll see what I'm wearing and they'll know it's true." A fresh tear slips over her lower left lid and creeps toward her chin.

"Okay." Joe rises from the barstool. He hands Irene another paper napkin and puts his other hand under Irene's elbow to steady her as she rises from her stool. "Waiter," he calls. Phil swivels his head in Joe's direction. "We're leaving now. Your money's on the counter. Thanks."

Phil makes the OK sign with his thumb and first finger, so as not to interrupt the old man, whose story is fascinating only to him.

"Let's go, Irene. I hope the police believe us." He opens the diner's door. They step out and turn left, heading along the sidewalk toward the glowing yellow light by the front door of the police station. It's only two short blocks away. Joe's insides seem to shrink as a pain shoots through his gut. They are only two short blocks from him either going to prison, or remaining a free man. What is he going to do?

Joe abruptly drops Irene's arm and bolts for the alley. Irene can face the police and all her fancy friends by herself. His butt is on the line, and he isn't going to jail for *any* broad, no matter how much fun she is, or how much he thinks he loves her. He is soon disappearing around the corner at the end of the alley.

Irene stares after him, her mouth a round "O" of surprise. But, moments later, she puts her hands on her hips, lifts her head high, and laughs loudly.

"Run, Joe. You'll get caught, especially after I report to the police what you did. Raping me and killing my husband. I won't tell them you did me the biggest favor of my life by killing that bastard Charles."

THE THIRTEENTH FLOOR

THE DOOR CLOSES as I survey the buttons on the panel in the wall. Yes, there is a floor thirteen. I know that many high rise buildings do not put a button numbered thirteen in their elevators. They skip the thirteenth floor and go directly from number twelve to number fourteen. I think this is extremely silly. If one were to stand outside the building and look up, counting the stories from the first to the top, she would undoubtedly count a thirteenth story. However, since I've never gotten off an elevator on the thirteenth floor, I decide to give it a try. Just to check, of course, to see if there really is a thirteenth floor. I gamely push the button.

Nothing happens. I push it again, this time holding it in for slightly longer. The elevator doesn't move, not even a budge. I press the button a third time with quick, short jabs of my forefinger. The car remains in place. I look all around at the paneled walls. I look up at the recessed tile ceiling. I see the camera high above in the corner, discreetly placed so as not to be observed. It has to be recording this, I think.

I wish now that I'd made the effort to hold open the door for the middle aged man in the rumpled suit hurrying across the lobby toward the elevator as the door closed. Then there'd be someone else who might know how to get it started. Barring that, I would at least have company.

Suddenly I begin to shake like a dog spitting up peach pits. My heart starts to pound like it's boxing its way out of my chest. My pulse races as if my blood is going to gush out of the veins in my wrists. My breath comes in gasps, much like a landed fish. I can't get enough air and I tear at the collar of my blouse, pulling it down and away from my straining throat.

I realize I'm having a panic attack and I'm reminded of the three I've had before. The first time was when I took a ride in a simulated space shuttle at Disney World's Epcot Center. I entered the four-seats-in-a-row capsule and sat in the second seat. My husband sat in the first. From the other side two children, whose ages were about ten and twelve, entered and sat in seats three and four. The doors locked, the air conditioner blew cold air, and the simulator lit up the dash in front of us. I began to feel as if I was accelerating directly to the heavens, and as I did, I began to hyperventilate. I closed my eyes, opened my mouth and took deep, slow breaths. I prayed the time would speed by and this trip would be over. I endured. That's all I could do. I simply sat with body rigid in my seat and prayed I didn't lose control completely and try to stand up and battle my way out. I made it to the end, but just barely. Another minute or so and I really don't know what means of escape I would've attempted.

The second time a panic attack attacked me was when I was lying back in the oral surgeon's chair being prepped for a root canal. I'd been administered the numbing shots to my gums and roof of my mouth. I'd had the rubber dam placed in my mouth to hold it open and to prevent any small file or tool that the doctor might drop from falling down my throat. The dentist applied the drill and bored out a small hole, but had not yet penetrated the pulp within the tooth. Abruptly I began to breathe heavily as if I couldn't get enough air. My heart raced and my blood pounded in my chest and veins. I began to sweat and to tremble. I felt tears roll from the corners of my eyes. All this happened within a matter of seconds. I told myself, "Gayle, get a grip. This is crazy. Just stop it!" Talking rationally to myself did absolutely no good. Nothing changed.

Tears were sliding down my cheeks as I motioned for him to remove the dam. He did. He listened to me haltingly explain that I was having a panic attack. He agreed, since he could see all my symptoms. I'd had several root canals before with no problems so he thought I'd be able to do it with a little help from a drug to calm me.

With drug ingested, I tried again three days later and got only as far as the shots before I asked him to stop. My tooth remains broken with a hole drilled in it.

The third attack occurred while I was unintentionally and inadvertently locked inside a tiny toilet stall in a cemetery in Russia. Some of the women on our tour elected to brave the primitive toilets, which were literally porcelain rimmed holes in the floor, and having experienced the Eastern type toilets on trips in the past, I joined them. The stench was almost over powering. I was tempted to hold my breath until I was finished. However, when I found that I couldn't get the door to open, the shallow breaths I'd forced myself to take were no longer an issue. I began to gasp for air. My heart raced, pumping my blood through my veins at double speed. Shaking helplessly, I tried pushing and kicking the door with no success. I increasingly felt like a pressure cooker ready to blow. I gave myself pep talks and tried to calm down while first one, then another, and yet another maintenance worker was brought in to try to free me. When they finally got the door open, I fell out of it and, on wobbly legs, rushed for the air outside.

The latest scare, aborted before it could mature into a monstrous panic, was at one of the University Centers housed in the sprawling football stadium complexes of a southern college known for its football program.

There to attend a social function in one of the ballrooms, an open door appeared in the bank of elevators and I entered along with my husband and another couple. I had no idea on which floor the function was being held. The couple seemed to know and pushed the floor button. Nothing happened. Another push, and still no movement. That's all it took for my heart to start racing, for my stomach to clench, for my throat to close so that I began to gasp for breath. However, this occurred in a matter of seconds, and in that same length of time the couple figured out the floor they had pushed the number for was inaccessible. I'd immediately started looking around the inside of the elevator, searching for any way to get out, when they then chose the correct floor after noticing the tiny note posted above the panel. The elevator rose swiftly and soundlessly, my heartbeat and breathing returned to normal, and my stomach unclenched. I was able to recover as quickly as the attack had started.

Now I'm here in this closet of an elevator with the walls closing in around me and the oxygen being leeched from the air and I'm ready to go ballistic. Is it because I pushed the button for the thirteenth floor? Maybe if I push the button for a different floor the thing will work. I slide my damp palms against the side seams of my skirt, drying them and my trembling fingers as much as I can on the slick material. I lift my arm and point my shaking finger at the button with twelve on it. My finger slips off. I only pressed one side of it, and that only slightly. I try again, this time aiming for the center of the two numerals that form twelve. I press hard and the elevator rises like a shot. The door whisks open on floor twelve to reveal a woman in very high heels tripping along the hallway and a harried man rushing toward the elevator with a sheaf of papers in his hands.

Immensely relieved, my trembling ebbs and I push the "hold door open" button so the man can enter. Should the goblins inhabiting the thirteenth floor act up on this ride, I will at the very least have someone with me to either help me battle them or to help me destroy this elevator in my efforts to get out. For get out of it, I most assuredly will!

I'll just continue to wonder what's on the thirteenth floor, not just in this building, but any thirteenth floor, for I will not again push a button for that mysterious floor. I flirted with the unknown and had a frightening experience. I figure I don't need to know.

A COLD DAY IN HELL

THE WINDOW IS shut to keep out the cold. Nearing it in her constant pacing, Ginger again begins to shiver. She's been shaking from the cold all day. The heat pump can do little to keep up with the penetrating cold that has descended out of nowhere with what seems like the wrath of Hell. "If only we had a little bit of Hell," she thinks. "At least we'd be a little warmer." Now she stands in front of the closed window and looks out at the banks of snow and the high drifts blown about by the wind, taking strange shapes as they are deposited in yet another location. She's never seen anything like this. Not in all of her twenty-three years. And not here in Florida, of all places. She stares, aghast and unbelieving, as a tall palm tree at the edge of her yard, where the lawn meets the beach, shudders and then sprawls across the snow dunes, falling with its weight of snow and ice, sending up plumes of cold mist into the icy air.

Yes, yes, the Green Peace activists and the other global warming talking heads had been warning not only the United States, but the entire world, about just this possibility for years. For decades, even.

But who knew? Who really could have guessed that the impossible would actually happen? She had been seeing tell-tale signs herself for some time now, but had chosen to play ostrich and stick her head in the sand and hope it would go away. She had almost literally done this. She had spent, and up until the last week, had continued to spend, hours on end walking the beautiful sand dunes here on the Gulf Coast of Florida. She sank her feet in the warm sugar sand and trailed her hands through the tall grassy sea oats that grew among the dunes and were a protected species along this stretch of the coast. One dare not uproot one or break off the wheat-like beards for fear of being seen, found out, and made an example of by the authorities. Just what they would do, other than to fine her, Ginger had never dared to find out.

Flying over the North Pole on their honeymoon trip to China, Ginger and Bud had witnessed the polar ice caps melting from their window seats in the airplane. Since it was such a long flight, they had asked for and received window seats each. Their plan was to lay their heads against the side of the plane and sleep, something those in the middle and aisle seats could not do. They had done this, each laying their head against a pillow and covering with a blanket and giving themselves over to Hypnos. Ginger's last glimpse of Bud before she succumbed to sleep was of his head lolling back and his mouth open while he took slow, deep breaths. She remembered thinking she was so glad that he didn't snore. Ginger soon was deep in a dream about their wedding day. The wedding itself, and the reception that followed, had made it a pretty much perfect day. Then Bud's insistent whisper aroused her.

"Ginger. Look, Ginger. Look out the window down there!"

At the urgency in his voice, Ginger awakened quickly. "What?"

"Look below us. Look at all the water. The ice caps are melting!"

Incredulous, Ginger pressed as much of herself as close to the window as she could. She gazed down curiously at the icescape below. Sure enough, the ice pack was shot through with what appeared to be running water. It looked like the ice was separating into huge fields with rivers bisecting them. "Oh, my Lord, how can that be?" she whispered. It seemed she had no breath to even say it aloud. To say she was shocked was a huge understatement. She was horrified. She wondered what this could mean for the world and its ability to survive.

There were other signs as well, those pointed out by the screaming dooms-day-ers, parleying their fears into hysteria on a massive scale in certain parts of the US and other countries. In the Rocky Mountains of not only the US, but of Canada as well, the "Green-niks" whipped the locals into a furiously frothing fever over the snow pack. Or the lack thereof. Not enough snow meant not enough melt, which meant not enough water. Which meant drought. Drought that affected all of life – from the humans to the animals, to the plants, to the fish and other seafood. Other places were tormented with too much snow. Experiencing one freak snow storm after another, the people were frenzied with fear of the snow melt and the resulting devastating floods.

Crowds marched in the capital cities of their home states and gathered in masses on the Mall in Washington, DC, hoping to attract enough attention with their sheer size and loud outcry for some answer to our problems with Mother Nature. They wrote letters by the thousands to their congressmen in futile attempts for somebody to do something. Talks. Meetings. More talks. More meetings. Global talks. Global meetings. Those in power, whether elected, appointed, or by monarchy rule, met and discussed ad nauseam the unimaginable problem facing our whole existence, but in the end, it was all just talk. No one had an answer. Nothing was done. Regions in the North continued to rarely experience snow or rain and were turning into arid deserts. People weathered the blistering heat as best they could, stripping to near nothing, and the skin cancer rates had already soared off the charts. The southern areas were cooling at an alarming rate and were now having snow storms and freezing precipitation of all kinds. Icy winds careened around corners, stinging and blinding the unlucky adventurer with the force of its frozen breath. The elderly and the very young were constantly at risk of perishing from either the blast-furnace-like heat or the appendage-numbing cold. Thousands already had done so.

So here Ginger is today, walking the floors of her Florida beach house, a place she has loved since childhood, and given to her as a wedding present by her maternal grandparents. They had gotten too old to fight the problems that living on the coast entail. Ginger thinks, "If only they knew!" Here she is, freezing in her coveted cottage, with snow blowing outside her closed window, covering the sand dunes and the beautiful white beaches. And she has no answers either. She will try with Bud, who is still asleep, wrapped in several quilts, in the adjacent bedroom which faces the ocean, to survive this unnatural onslaught. She will bundle up and try to stay warm, and she will pray that we are not entering another ice-age, which would bring certain death because the modern world is not acclimated to anything near such cold. Or, perhaps, the complete reversal, a searing, parching, withering heat that would burn the very life out of everything. Then all life would cease on Earth.

Ginger suddenly feels stifled, as if she can't catch her breath. She quickly raises open the window and takes huge gasps of icy cold, freezing air into her lungs. She gazes at the frozen landscape, at the snow drifts that once were sand dunes. As she lowers the window, she wonders how much more of this craziness this world can endure. How much longer we can possibly survive in it. And if survival is an option at all.

"Ginger. Ginger." She cocks her head, her ear turned toward the bedroom where Bud is sleeping. It comes again, this time marginally louder: "Gin-gerrrrr . . . ."

"What on Earth?" Ginger thinks, moving quickly across the room and into the bedroom where Bud is leaning over the side of the bed, his lower half still surrounded by bedcovers now in total disarray. He is weakly heaving into a spreading stain on the floor. He looks up, his face ghostly white and his eyes streaked a devilish red

"I'm sorry, Honey," he gasps. "It just came on so quickly until I couldn't make it out of bed."

"Let me look at you, Sweetie," Ginger says as she lays a hand on his forehead. No need for a temperature thermometer. His skin is scorching to the touch. She says, "Be right back," and hurries to the bathroom for a cold washcloth to put on his forehead. It's a good thing it is cold water she is looking for, since the warm water with which she plans to wet another washcloth to wipe his face never materializes.

Putting an arm around Bud, Ginger eases him back onto the bed where he lies, taking shuddering breaths against his pillows. She applies the cold washcloth to his forehead and wipes his parched lips with the dry one. Frantically, she wonders what to do. The phone lines have been down for a couple of days already, so she can't call the local pharmacist for his advice. The nearest hospital is forty miles away, and forty minutes on a good day. "Forty miles may as well be four thousand with the way the roads are right now," Ginger thinks. Throughout the early afternoon, Ginger applies the cold washcloths to Bud's head, and stripping his pajamas from him, she applies cold, wet towels to his entire body. Immediately, they warm and she imagines them sending tendrils of steam toward the ceiling of the bedroom. Repeatedly, he weakly regurgitates ever-redder bile into the galvanized bucket Ginger places bedside.

"I've got to do something!" Ginger rails aloud. "I've got to get him to a doctor." She thinks of the jet skis sitting benignly in the garage and tries to figure some way she could get them to work out of the water and on the snow. With her mouth in a tight line, she realizes it's impossible. The Jet Ski has a rotor, and that wouldn't work in the snow. She pictures the walls of the garage and all the items crowding its floor. She sees the row boat and pictures dragging Bud's heavy body into it and her manning the oars. Nope, she can't row through the snow.

She resumes her pacing in front of the picture window that is now almost filled with white, blowing fluffiness, and watches the heavy snow and howling wind do their tricks. Coltishly, she jumps when a large slide of snow slips from the roof the short distance to the snow dune that all but obscures her front door.

"That does it!" Ginger mutters through clinched teeth. She strides purposely across the floor to open the inside door to the garage. Her eyes scan the room, her brain flaring with hope at each new possibility and then guttering out at the impossibility that quickly followed.

Her eyes alight upon the long body of a surf board. "Oh," she says. Just a small, quiet "Oh." She purses her lips in thought. "I could put Bud on the surf board and pull him," she thinks. "But, what will I use to walk through the snow?" She continues glancing about the garage, looking for the perfect answer. She finds it in the form of two of her Grandpa's gut-strung tennis rackets. Old and brittle, but even so, the strings were definitely meant for long-term use.

She races back into the bedroom and finds Bud pale and lethargic. "Bud, I know how we're going to get you to the doctor, or at least the pharmacist in town. You have to help me all you can. I need you to bundle up in your blankets and you need to get to the garage somehow. We're going to tie you on the surf board and I'm going to pull you to the pharmacy. It's only about five blocks. I know we can make it."

"How are you going to do that?" Bud croaks.

"I'm going to use Grandpa's old tennis rackets as snowshoes." Ginger laughs aloud at the absurdity of the situation, but inside she feels hope that it might actually work. She heads back to the garage and locates the shovel used for digging in the flower garden. Using the inside garage door handle to ease up the door, she immediately has to fight back the snow that attempts to fall inside. With back-breaking lifts, she urgently makes headway against the piling snow to make an exit path from the garage. She looks toward the house door to see Bud standing wrapped in blankets looking ever-so-much like the Michelin Man.

"Here, let me put these on," indicating the tennis rackets and the roll of thick, rope-like twine on the workbench. She places her foot in the middle of the racket and quickly loops the twine around and around her foot and racket. She repeats this with the other racket and twine.

Wresting the heavy surf board from its secured spot tires her rapidly, but Ginger hurries to place it on the floor and, grabbing Bud, she helps him to lie down on it. Finally she has him on it and, lifting first the top end and then the bottom end, she wraps and wraps lengths of rope around Bud and the board. She snags her Grandpa's gardening gloves and puts them on Bud's shaking fingers. Scanning the workshop area of the garage, she finds another pair of Grandpa's work gloves, stiff and much too big, but pulls them on her hands. She then loops another length of rope around and through Bud's hands and ties it around her waist, after threading it through the belt loops of her jeans. She checks her jeans pocket to see if she has her cell phone and hopes that it will find a signal if she gets into a dire emergency out there in all that deep snow. The last thing she does is stuff herself inside a rain slicker she finds hanging on a peg and hopes it, along with the heavy sweaters she has donned, will hold up to the task of keeping her from freezing to death.

Ginger heaves a huge sigh, flips the slicker's hood over her head, and leans into the wind and the rapidly piling snow at the garage's entrance. She pulls with all her might. Bud and the surf board slide onto the snow and continue to follow behind her as she forces one foot in front of the other. She passes the snow-shrouded trees and shrubbery of her property, unrecognizable as such now, and continues to pull. Her breath freezes in the air as it jets from her mouth. One foot in front of the other. One more time. Pull. Pull. Pull. Her mind goes on auto-pilot as she repeats this mantra over and over again. She falls. She gets up slowly. She is so winded she can hardly catch her breath. The muscles of her arms, back and shoulders are on fire. Her leg muscles are screaming. She falls again. While she is on her knees she checks on Bud. He is sliding off the surf board as it lists to the right. She crab-crawls in the snow and pushes him back on. She rises and continues to pull.

She passes more humps and blobs and moments later she realizes that one of them is the top of a red stop sign. The red stop sign just one block from the pharmacy. The only drugstore this little nook on the Gulf coast possesses. Doubts now flood her mind. She begins to fear the pharmacy is closed. Dread shoots an icy needle throughout her straining heart. But then she remembers. The druggist lives above the drugstore. Another icy spear spirals inward. What if the druggist has already fled from this abominable weather?

The druggist is at home. He is standing by his second-story window and sees Ginger approach, an apparition appearing from the blinding white. He races down the stairs and thanks his lucky stars that he has just been down to clear the doorway for just such an emergency as this. He helps to untie Bud from his makeshift transport and yells for his wife to come running and to bring a bottle of Wild Turkey with her.

The druggist liberally pours a shot down Bud's throat and hands the bottle to Ginger to take a swig. Bud coughs, gags, gasps, but manages to keep it down, his teeth chattering uncontrollably. Ginger licks her lips, savoring the fire burning its way to her belly.

She explains the symptoms to the doctor. The doctor calls his teenage son to help him get Bud upstairs to a bed and immediately turns to go back downstairs to plunder his medicine supply. The druggist's wife, who has settled for nothing less than a gas range, plies Ginger with hot chicken noodle soup. Bud, feverish and unable to get warm, tries a few trickles, but retches loudly, and no more is offered him. The druggist doses him with a vile-looking liquid and he soon drifts into a fitful sleep.

It is now the second day at the druggist's home and Ginger stands in front of the big second-story window and looks out at the white swirling snow that shows no signs of abating. Nothing is moving in the sea of white. The snow now covers the bottom third of this second-story window, allowing her to see from its top the village appearing as a snow-scape, now blanketed in a sea of white, covering streets, cars, houses. Everything is covered, and she knows that soon, this building, the tallest in town, will be covered as well. "How did this happen?" Ginger wonders for the millionth time.

Bud is somewhat improved, but still pale and shaky. She doubts that he, indeed any of them, will survive this horror of catastrophic proportions. But the will to survive is strong, so she hopes someone with some kind of knowledge and experience can come up with some kind of solution. Whatever miracle that might be. And soon. Very, very soon.

WE SHOULD HAVE KNOWN BETTER

"**W**E SHOULD HAVE known better." Judy stated it emphatically. "I can't believe we actually fell for it."

"I can't, either," Anne replied, sounding just about as disgusted as one could be.

Judy and Anne were both recently divorced after what seemed like a lifetime of marriage for each of them. For Anne, it was thirty years, and for Judy, it was thirty-three. Both had been married during their college years when they were young and starry-eyed and thought that love would last forever. Not so. So now they were on a road trip and enjoying the camaraderie that only old-time friends share.

They drove from their side-by-side homes in Virginia, where the lawn between their houses was literally worn down into a discernible path from where their feet had trod upon it for two decades. Now, husbandless and fancy free, they had set out for an adventure.

They were riding along, enjoying the beautiful scenery of West Virginia, when Judy exclaimed, "Good gosh, I didn't know Falling Water was this close to us."

"What?" Anne asked. She had been paying attention to the roadwork just ahead. "What are you talking about?"

"Falling Water. Frank Lloyd Wright's Falling Water. You know, that big house he built with the waterfall falling down right inside it."

"Oh, right. Where did you say it was?"

"I don't know exactly, but I saw the sign right back there. You just passed it."

"You want to go see it? We've got all the time in the world, so a little detour won't hurt anything."

"Yes, I'd really like to see it. Turn around and let's go back and check the sign."

Anne turned the car around at the next side road and they were soon back and gazing at the sign. Sure enough, a green, metal highway sign announced Falling Water was at the next turn-off. They proceeded to the turn-off and drove up a gently inclining hill. Cresting it, they found a small town lying below. From their position above the town, they looked for anything that might possibly be Falling Water.

"Well, I don't see it," Judy said. "Maybe it's back behind there in some woods, or something."

"Come on, we'll drive down and look around for it," Anne decided.

They drove slowly through the small town and waved at several people they saw along the way. One lady was inspecting the contents of her mailbox, and still, at mid-day, was wearing her pajamas and robe. Even so, she turned to wave and to watch them drive by. They received another wave from an elderly man who rocked in his high-backed rocker on his tiny front porch. They saw other people out and about, but they did not see Falling Water.

"Maybe we should stop and ask someone how to find it," Judy said.

"Okay, I'll pull into that hardware store parking lot just up ahead. Certainly somebody in there will know where it is."

Anne slid the Jeep into the parking spot nearest the door that didn't have a "Reserved for Handicapped" sign. "I'll go ask," she volunteered, opening her car door and stepping out.

"Wait, I'm coming, too," Judy said, and proceeded to wrestle with the Jeep's door handle until she finally got it open.

"I know; I'll get it repaired, I promise. I should've done it before we left on this trip."

"Right," Judy snorted, blue eyes blazing.

They entered the store, which was woefully empty at this time of day. They both wondered how such a store as this stayed in business in a small town. From the looks of it, it must have been tough to do so.

Anne offered a friendly smile as she approached the counter where the lone clerk lazily flipped through a magazine. Looking at it upside down, she could see it was a parts magazine. She looked around and decided he was wasting his time; there were already too many parts sitting on the crowded shelves.

"Hi," she said. "We were just passing through and we saw the sign on the highway for Falling Water and decided to stop. We don't know where it is and there aren't any signs directing us to it. We hoped that you might be able to help us find it."

The young man's blank blue eyes gazed back at her, confusion written on his face.

"What?"

"Falling Water," Judy responded, wondering who this idiot was. "The house built by the architect Frank Lloyd Wright. The sign on the highway said it was here."

"Where?" Again, the blue-eyed bewilderment.

"Right here," Judy said. "It's a big house with a waterfall in it. Do you know where it is?"

"Ohhh, – yes." It seemed understanding had dawned on him. His eyes lit up, a smile appeared on his face and his furrowed brow relaxed. "It's down the road a piece. Go back out to the road and then turn to your right and keep going for about a mile. You'll see it up on the left, sitting on a hill."

"Thanks for your help," Anne said, and they left the store, eager to get on with their trip to Falling Water.

Anne drove for more than a mile and they saw nothing remotely resembling what they were looking for. They continued for another mile and turned around and drove back, diligently searching both sides of the road for any sign of Falling Water. None was to be found anywhere.

With a frown between her eyes and her lips pursed in thought, Anne suddenly turned to Judy, who was still searching the roadside and hills with less and less enthusiasm. "Hey, are you sure Falling Water is here in West Virginia? Now that I think about it, I remember seeing a special on it on TV and I believe they said it was in Pennsylvania."

"Oh, my God, I think you're right!"

"Yeah, I'm pretty sure that I am. I can't believe I didn't remember this earlier before we wasted all this time searching for it."

"And the nerve of that guy at the hardware store. Lying to us like that!"

Anne just had to laugh. "Don't you know he had a grand time teasing us? I wonder if he does it all the time, or if we were the first tourists stupid enough to think Falling Water was here."

"We should have known better. I can't believe we actually fell for it."

"I can't either."

"You know what?" Judy asked with a hint of glee in her voice.

"What?"

"What do you think about us driving on up to Pennsylvania and going to the real Falling Water?"

"That's a fantastic idea, Judy! We should stop for some lunch and get out the map and plan our route. Does McDonald's sound all right to you?"

"Right on," Judy said, excitement shading her voice.

They had set out to visit a friend in Ohio, but over chicken McNuggets and diet cokes, they decided to abandon that plan for now. Their new plan was to return to Interstate 68 at Morgantown, West Virginia, and then to take Route 43 through Uniontown, Pennsylvania, and head on up to Connellsville. From there, it would only be fifteen or twenty miles to their destination of the real Falling Water.

"I believe, short of Norway, this is the prettiest scenery I have ever seen," Judy declared, gazing out the window.

"Ah, Norway was something, wasn't it?"

The two good friends had, a dozen years ago, taken a trip to Scandinavia and loudly proclaimed in every country they visited that it was truly the most beautiful they had seen. However, they both could agree that Norway stood in a class unto itself. The soaring mountains with the thousands of both big and small waterfalls cascading down them were a sight to behold. Then the fjords at their bottom where the cascades descended into the watery depths were cold beauty at its finest.

After a couple of hours driving time, during which they thoroughly enjoyed West Virginia's, Maryland's, and Pennsylvania's scenery, Judy exclaimed, "I see the sign!"

"Are you sure it is the correct sign for the correct Falling Water?" Anne teased.

"Oh, you . . . Stop bugging me about that! It says Fallingwater – all one word."

After parking the car and getting their first real look at the magical place, they were at first speechless.

Then, "Ohhhh," they both sighed in unison.

This unimaginably glorious home did have a waterfall flowing through it. They found out that the family wanted Wright to build a house near the falls, but he, using the brilliance that it seemed only he possessed, drew a plan with the waterfall inside the house. The owners were so taken with the novelty of the idea that they immediately said for him to start his project. Start it he did, and it was completed in 1939.

The pair wandered among the rooms marveling at the sparseness of furniture and the angular surfaces used throughout Wright's signature homes. Both the living and bedroom levels were shored up with concrete trays that cantilevered over the waterfall's stream.

"Amazing," Anne reverently said.

"Simply breathtaking," Judy added.

They completely toured the unusual home and its surroundings and took rolls of pictures. Satisfied, they returned to the Jeep and once more set out on their adventure.

Anne snickered and asked, "Now, do you suppose you might be able to find us a Disneyland to visit on our way to Ohio, Judy?"

Judy's rather vehement response, something about foot inserted into nether regions, was drowned by the sound of the Jeep's engine starting and Anne's loud laughter.

THE JOB OF A LIFETIME

DAHLIA WAKES TO the softly playing music of her alarm. She detests loud, rude noises invading her senses. She languorously stretches her long limbs, her white arms reaching high over her head. Her toes reach for the end of the bed as she twists first one limb, then the next, enjoying this delicious stretching of her tired muscles. She had a late night following a strenuous workout at the gym. She can't imagine, but is thankful for, how her body manages to get into the positions that it does. A smile plays upon her face as she examines that perfect body, now highlighted by the sunlight streaming through the wide bedroom window, which soars high into the sky above the bustling city. In her profession, a toned, perfect, beautiful body is a must. And an agile one is always a plus.

She heads for the bath where she will soap and sponge and mist away the residue of her past evening. Stopping at her medicine cabinet that holds birth control pills and douches along with scented soaps, bubble baths, silken powders and delicately scented body sprays, she chooses the assortment she needs for her ablution. She starts the water flowing in the tub and pours in a generous stream of white ginger-scented bath oil. The tub continues to fill as she returns to her closet to select which delectable outfit she will wear today. A sexy short dress and lacy, gossamer panties are her standard costume for her evenings. However, for her days, which belong only to her, and for which she fights valiantly to keep only hers, she is free to choose something comfortable and a shade less sexy. But, she is a beautiful woman with a beautiful body and she has to adhere to the unwritten female code: If you've got it; flaunt it. So she selects a classic pair of white capris and a multi-colored strapless top of bold fuchsia and magenta flowers, to be held up by her magnificent breasts. No bra needed.

Stepping to her bureau, she opens the top drawer, gazes at the delicate bikini panties, and chooses a pair made of the softest silk in muted beige so they won't show through her white capris. Back to the cavernous closet she goes, and this time she selects a pair of spectacular shoes to accompany the ensemble. Hot-pink espadrilles with strings to tie around her slender ankles.

Dahlia returns to the bath where the tub is now filled, perfumed bubbles hovering above it. She slips into her ears the buds with which she will listen to soft, classical music, steps over the rim and eases her lush body into its warm depths. "Ahhhh, peace," she whispers. She lays her head back against the headrest attached to the tub and closes her eyes in contentment.

The phone is ringing as she steps from her bath. Lazily, she wraps a soft towel around her curves and unhurriedly answers it in a husky voice. "Dahlia."

"Dahlia, where have you been? I've been calling you for half an hour. We have an important party for you tonight," her employer's deceptively girlish voice trills. "He's a company CEO from out of town who will be here only for the one night. He's asked for someone with your particular skills. With his expectations, not to mention his assets, we certainly wouldn't want to disappoint him, now would we?" Not giving Dahlia a chance to answer, she continues, "You're meeting him at the bar in the lounge of The Four Seasons Hotel at eleven o'clock tonight."

Dahlia sighs and puts the phone back in its charger and dons today's outfit. She hasn't yet eaten so she enters the kitchen in search of something light. She settles on a green salad and spritzes it with balsamic vinegar mixed with light olive oil. While daintily eating it, she assesses in her mind her repertoire of evening wear, trying to isolate the most promising of the barely-there dresses hanging like pretty maids all in a row in her closet.

She thinks she has hit on the very one she needs for this evening's activities. It falls just above the knee, has a wide, flared skirt that hangs in pleasing folds from its tiny, cinched waist. With a draped, scooped neckline, it is both demure and sexy at once, as just the tops of her breasts are exposed. Thin straps cross the shoulders from back to front where they disappear into the folds of the neckline. Best of all, it is red. Tonight's heels will also be red with spaghetti straps crisscrossing her lightly tanned toes and a strap around each ankle.

Padding across her thick carpet in her bare feet to her closet, Dahlia stoops to snare the pink espadrilles. She inserts her feet and then sits upon the end of her bed to tie them about her thin calves. After smoothing the bed's silk comforter, and pushing her slender arm through the straps of the ridiculously expensive Gucci bag, she descends to the street below for a mind-freeing shopping foray in which she can lose herself and her obligations. After a few fun-filled hours, she returns with her arms surrounding shopping bags filled to overflowing with books and puzzles and an arresting portrait of a young woman that reminds her of her mother. Today was a day for not thinking about her job. This was a day for Dahlia's alter ego.

Again she enters the bathroom for a refreshing shower before leaving for work. Dahlia soaps a bath sponge until the suds are literally sprouting from it and slides it sensuously over her body. She washes her hair with an expensive salon shampoo and applies the conditioner. Last, she reaches for the disposable douche and administers it to her body. She likes to be scrupulously clean; this insures that she is.

Standing before her mirror, she lifts her heavy tresses atop her head. She would wear it up tonight, adding to the mystique. Her long, light brown hair has a hint of wave shot through it, and it will look slightly tousled when she unpins it later.

She massages jell through her hair before gently blowing it dry. Gathering it in both hands, she winds it into a fetching knot upon her head, allowing a few tendrils to escape the confining combs she artfully places on either side of the twisted tresses. Satisfied with the finished look, she chooses a perfume suitable for this evening's work. She lifts the shimmering bottle and lightly sprays the back of her neck, between her breasts, the inside of each wrist, and finishes with a quick jet to her shaved and nearly nude pubic mound. Dahlia applies a smattering of a lightly scented powder to the insides of her thighs to be sleek and silky to the touch.

Smelling delicious, she pads to the bureau for her bikini panties. She slips a long leg into each leg hole and slides them up her body. Crossing to the closet, she inspects the red dress with approval, and raises it high above her head, then lets it float down her body. Reaching behind, her talented fingers locate the zipper, and with a quick tug, she glides it up her back. Pirouetting in front of the mirror, she admires the striking figure she sees in it.

And now for her makeup: She applies a light foundation that enhances her natural skin color, and artistically paints mauve eye shadow on her eyelids as a painter might to a canvas. No artifice is needed to give her cheeks color. She adds mascara with the flip of a wand to her eyelashes.

With a final swipe of a red-tinged lip gloss, she is picture perfect. She ferrets from her dresser drawer the little red sequined purse that contains a small mirror, a lip gloss tube, a tissue, and five twenties. Mama said never to leave home without money, and this is one tip that Dahlia always obeys.

Dahlia sweeps into the lounge at one minute to eleven, attracting the attention of every male there. She is stunning and she knows it. She stalks to the bar, head up and chest forward, hips swaying ever-so-seductively. Her eyes sweep the room as she purposefully approaches the bar stools. She slips a hip onto one and faces the bartender. "A glass of white wine, please."

Out of the corner of her eye she sees a man rise from his seat at a table and head toward her. "Oh, please, don't let this slob be him," she silently pleads. The man sits down beside her on the right. Dahlia starts to turn toward him when she feels a presence behind her left shoulder. Hoping the CEO would be anybody except the guy on her right, Dahlia lifts her questioning face to the person to her left.

"You must be my sister-in-law. I've been waiting to meet you."

These words stun Dahlia's brain for a moment until she figures out that it is just a line the man is using to help her in an awkward situation.

"Yes, I believe I am," Dahlia responds, all the while thinking that this guy looks vaguely familiar. "I understand that you are now the CEO of your company," she continues, fishing to see if he is her client for the evening.

"Yep, I just got promoted." He grins down at Dahlia, showing white teeth in a pleasant face.

"That's quite an accomplishment. Perhaps we should celebrate."

Taking her arm and helping her from the bar stool, he said, "Right. That's a great idea. Let's go burst a bottle of champagne and get to know each other, sister-in-law."

He escorts her toward the elevator, hand held solicitously under her elbow. Inside, he punches the button for the twenty-second floor. He turns to look at her and his gaze lingers while he looks thoughtful, but he doesn't say anything. The elevator rises like a shot and they are walking out onto the twenty-second floor in a matter of seconds. He inserts the door card key and ushers her into the opulence The Four Seasons is noted for. She sees a white envelope on the desk that appears to be bulging with cash. Most pay with credit cards these days, she thought.

He goes to the room's bar where he nonchalantly plucks from its ice bath the bottle of Dom Perignon champagne he'd earlier ordered. "Have a seat, please," he offers with a sweep of his hand toward the inviting couch. Dahlia does, spreading the folds of her dress around her.

Placing a handy towel around its neck and detangling the wires holding in the cap, he opens it with both thumbs pressing hard against the cork. Predictably, the cork flies toward the ceiling and the champagne's aroma fills the air as a stream of foam glides down the side of the bottle. He pours two glasses of the shimmering, golden wine and turns to Dahlia. He places one tall, cool flute in her hand and salutes her, "To you, my lovely companion." Dahlia smiles and sips the cold, crisp wine with its tiny bubbles bursting under her nose as he takes a gulp and grins at her. Silently they sip from their glasses as they frankly assess each other. Finally, the client sets his glass down. Dahlia follows suit.

Smiling, she sways toward him and raises her arms to place them around his neck. She looks up at him, now a slight smile playing on her full lips, and says, "I'm here to make your evening an unforgettable one. What would you like me to do? Or who would you like me to be? I'll be and do whatever you want." She raises an eyebrow suggestively as she says this last line.

He bends his head down to her and sweeps her tight against him. His mouth descends on hers and he kisses her thoroughly and expertly. Dahlia returns his kiss, surprised at his skill and surprising herself at her response to him.

"What can I do for you?" Dahlia asks breathlessly with her head back, looking up at him. Her hands stray to his belt buckle and expertly divest him of the cincher. Her fingers play up and down the length of his zipper, feeling the growing bulge hidden there.

"Let me undress you." He turns her around and unzips her zipper, allowing the floating dress to pool at her feet. His hands move to her naked breasts, which he cradles as he gently rubs his thumbs across the pink-tinged nipples. He bends his head and captures a nipple in his mouth, tonguing it in swirls. Dahlia gasps and feels a pain of desire shoot across her abdomen. He reluctantly moves his mouth from her breast to look in her eyes as his hands slide down her sides to the impediment of her bikini line. He hooks his thumbs and first fingers in the waistband of the sheer panties and slowly slips them down her long legs. He presses his face against her abdomen, his lips nuzzling her soft folds. Never has she been aroused so instantly by any client. Certainly, there were a few who were talented lovers and whom she enjoyed. But this is different, she thinks. It's almost like I know what to expect. Trembling in anticipation, she gently tugs his head and he rises to encircle her body with his and to drop another searing kiss on her lips. Reaching down, he cradles each foot as he slips free the straps holding on the spiked-heel sandals.

"Let me undress you now," Dahlia whispers on an exhale. She unzips his zipper, which is now no easy job as it has to move over and around a large obstacle blocking its way. Finished with the trousers, she lets them fall to the floor at his feet. She loosens his tie and removes it slowly, eyes holding fast on his. Her fingers expertly coax the shirt buttons through their holes until she is able to strip it from his broad shoulders. She bends to remove his shoes, first untying the laces, then slipping off each one, then his socks. He steps out and away from his trousers, standing in just his white jockey shorts. Dahlia smiles in eager anticipation. Hooking her long red nails into the waistband, she slowly peels them down his muscular legs, while gazing at what was once hidden beneath the shorts. She reaches up with both hands and frees her hair from their combs. As it tumbles down her back and on to her shoulders, almost obscuring one breast, his eyes darken and he reaches for her again.

"Now, let me love you," he whispers, as he lifts her in his arms and lowers her onto the bed. Dahlia finds she has little to do since he is already well aroused and he has taken control of the session. So often she has to do everything. It seems the clients think they have paid for it, so why should they work for it? The tables were turning and Dahlia couldn't be happier. They continue with foreplay designed to make both eager for consummation.

"What's your name?" she asks him on a gasp as he enters her.

"Edward. What's yours?"

"Susan." She is shocked to hear her real name coming out of her mouth. Why on earth did she do that, she wonders.

He looks down at her, grins, and says, "Hello, Susan."

There was no coherent talking after that. Just moans and gasps and short directives like "There." "That's it." And, of course, "Oh, God."

Their quivering bodies come to a stop, all needs sated. Edward tucks her against his side with her head on his chest. He idly plays with a long strand of her hair, fingering its softness.

Dahlia elevates herself on her elbow and looks into his face. Her eyes search his as she asks, "Do I know you, Edward?"

"I think you might."

"Tell me how."

"It's no cloak and dagger situation, Susan. It's really quite simple."

"And . . . ?"

"I thought you looked familiar to me when I saw you walk into the lounge."

"I thought you were vaguely familiar, too." Her sculpted eyebrows draw down in consternation. "But how?"

"I think you were a couple of grades behind me in school."

"Oh, my God," Dahlia says, sitting up abruptly. "That can't be."

"Well, I've changed a bit. And you have certainly changed a bit. That is, if you are the same Susan Graham that went to Homestead High when I was going there."

Dahlia puts her face in her hands and starts to sob. "Oh, I can't believe it."

"Why are you crying, Susan?" He takes her again into his arms and holds her close.

"Because I hoped no one would ever find me here. I got away from that small town in the only way I could. I never had any money growing up, but I found I could make a ton of it here, doing this." She looks down at her splendid, naked body and gestures at it with her hands.

"I left Homestead when I graduated, too. You still had a couple of years left in school at that time. The point is that when I left, I did so in order to make something of myself. I went to college and then got an entry level job with my firm. It's been fourteen years, but I finally worked my way up to CEO of my company. It's rather small, but I'm very proud of it and the work we do. I was here in the big city and decided to try a hooker . . ." He pauses and says, "Sorry, Susan," and then continues. "So, you are the one they sent me. I had no idea I would know you." He stops and peers into her eyes. "Did you recognize me, Susan?"

Dahlia shakes her head no. "I thought I might have seen you before, but never," she pauses, clears her throat, and tries again, "never as a client. I'd certainly remember that."

"So what do we do now?"

"You go home to your wife and I continue giving men a night they'll never forget."

"I don't have a wife."

Incredulous, Dahlia asks, "You aren't married?"

"No. I never met anyone who wanted to work with me to get where I wanted to be. I've done it alone. I'm thirty-six years old; I've worked hard every day of my life, and I just wanted a diversion to cap off my hard-earned promotion." Grinning, Edward says, "You are that diversion, Susan, and I have to say, based on what just happened between us, you are one hell of a diversion!"

Dahlia smiles, then says, "It's almost time for me go." She rises from the bed and looks for the wisp of bikini panties lying on the floor near the foot of the bed. The sexy red dress she finds near the desk. She dons the panties, pushing through one long, shapely leg at a time, while Edward watches, naked, from the bed. She steps into the dress, but before she can reach behind her to zip it, Edward is at her back, laying a row of scorching kisses along her spine. He deftly zips the dress and turns her around. Raising his hand, he sweeps back a lock of hair from her forehead. Bending his head to hers, he kisses her long and deeply.

"I'll be back again," he says. He walks to the desk and picks up the heavy white envelope. "This is for you."

"I'd like to have you as a client," Dahlia says, once again all business. Swiftly, she opens the door and is through it and gone in but a moment. Edward watches her adopt her professional manner and provocatively sway down the hallway.

Susan exits The Four Seasons Hotel, gives the doorman a nod, and stands at the curb while he hails a cab for her. It is four o'clock in the morning. Dahlia's job is over until deep into the coming night. For now she is content to be Susan and to relish her memories of this night. A night when she really wasn't Dahlia at all.

SEEING THE LIGHT

THE LIGHT IS blindingly bright. Liz opens her eyes and sees she is looking down a long passageway at the light coming from its end. Alarmed, she wonders what it is.

She looks down at a body lying on an operating table. Holy crap! It is her! *If that is her*, she thinks, *then where in the hell is the real her?*

A quick search of the room reveals that she is both places, on the table and here, hovering above.

I can't be two people, Liz thinks.

She listens to the talk among the doctors huddled around her bed.

"We're losing her, Dr. Smith!"

"Quick, use the paddles, Doctor Jones!"

Liz sees the body beneath her jerk.

"Still no heartbeat. Do it again."

While she watches her other body spasm, her new body floats to a corner of the room.

She looks across the ceiling and cries, "My God! Mom? Is that really you?" Her long dead mother sits in a wooden chair, hovering just below the ceiling.

"Yes, Lizzie. It's me. I've come to comfort you and to guide you through the light.

"But, I'm not ready to go, Mom! I'm only thirty-six years old, for God's sake!"

"It's okay, Honey. It won't hurt at all."

"Hey, it looks like we've got a rhythm again!" one of the doctors yells.

"Yes, it looked like she was a goner, for sure. But she's got a long way to go before she's out of the woods."

Maybe they're actually going to save me, Liz thinks. *I need to make Mom see that I don't want to go with her.*

"Mom, I love you and I always will, but I'm just not ready to go with you yet."

"We'll see. I'll wait right here in case you need me." She tips her chair back and prepares to wait.

Liz dares to sneak a peek at the light at the end of the hallway. It isn't as bright as before.

"We're finished with the hysterectomy. Doctor Jones, would you close for me, please?"

"Yes, of course. However, I'm still worried about losing her."

"You're right. We've got to do something, because her heart rate is much too slow. She's got to be more reactive to the meds. If not, she may not wake up at all."

"Not reactive? People, I'm right here!" But, not one of the doctors looks up to where Liz hovers.

The light grows dimmer still.

"Hey, look up here. Here I am!"

"Uh-oh, she's crashing again!"

The light grew brighter again. "It's almost time, Lizzie," her mom said.

"No, I won't go! I'm going to survive! I'm going to get back in that body, and I'll see you again when it's truly my time."

"Wow!" Doctor Smith said. "I've never seen anyone fight like this before. How can she do this when she's not even conscious?"

"Yes, her numbers are rising. I think she just might make it. And you never know why someone can fight for survival even when they're sedated and not aware of what's happening to them."

Liz finishes inserting herself into the figure lying on the table.

"She's coming around!"

Liz looks for the hallway and the light is so dim she can barely see it.

She closes her eyes; she is so very tired from the near death experience, and she sleeps.

When she awakes again, she is lying in a hospital bed with bandages on her stomach. There is no one near the ceiling. The passageway and light are totally gone. She smiles and says, "I'll join you when I'm ready, Mom. Just not yet."

MORT AND MEGAN MAKE MAGIC

"**O**H, MEGAN, SHE'S beautiful!" Mort exclaimed. He appraised her further, squinting his eyes, wrinkling his forehead, and pursing his lips. "She looks just like my Uncle Sid," he announced.

"She does not," laughed Megan, holding her newborn baby daughter up and away from the long incision the doctor had made in her abdomen when delivering the baby. She was a big baby and Megan had not dilated enough to deliver her vaginally. It had to be a Caesarean Section delivery. "She's her own cute self. She doesn't look like anybody, yet," Megan protested, "least of all your very Jewish Uncle Sid."

As Mort settled on the side of the hospital bed, he jostled her.

"Ouch!" she said, placing a hand against her stomach. "You have to not only be careful with the baby, but with me, as well. The nurse says it will take several days for my incision to lose most of its soreness."

"Okay. Sorry." Mort gave Megan his very best doe-eyed look, guaranteed to melt her heart, and to garner her forgiveness, at the very least. "Let's check and see if all her equipment is there," he said, peeling away the blankets the nurse had wrapped her in. He looked at her tiny feet and counted toes. "Ten," Mort affirmed. "Ten toes to match her fingers."

He slipped back the sticky tape holding her diaper around her minute little bottom and said, "And we're sure she's a girl? I'm telling you, she looks like my Uncle Sid." Finished pulling the diaper off, he looked and made certain that he had, indeed, fathered a daughter. "Yep, she's a girl. Even though she really does like an old man."

"Put her diaper back on!" Megan admonished. "Her little bottom will freeze, hanging out of her diaper in this freezing cold room. Why on Earth they have the air conditioning turned to where it reads "Perma Frost," I'll never understand."

Mort took the baby from Megan's arms and laid her at the end of the bed. There he diapered her in a clean, and to him a tiny, scrap of cotton and plastic. "Geez, these things could fit a doll. Hey, maybe we can name her Dolly," he quipped as he finished wrapping her in her pink blanket. He carefully picked up the baby from the end of the bed and balanced her in his arms.

Taking him seriously, Megan thought quickly before she hedged her reply, "Oh, I don't know Mort. I thought we might give her a family name. I don't think anyone on either side is named Dolly."

Mort burst out laughing at the serious look on Megan's face. "I was just joking about naming her Dolly, Megan," he gasped out between guffaws. Slowing his laughter to just a smile, he added, "But, a family name would be nice. Maybe Sidney spelled with a 'Y'?" His smile got bigger and bigger until he was again laughing. This upset the baby in his arms and she began to cry. He swiftly handed her back to Megan whose arms were already reaching for her.

"No, no, no, and no! I will not have my daughter named after your Uncle Sid, no matter how you spell it!" She grinned at him to soften her words, just in case he was not just joking about this name, as he had said he was about naming her Dolly. "Family name or not," she added.

Now over his laughing fit, Mort said, "Seriously though, Honey, what do you really want to name her? I know we considered several names, but she really doesn't look like a Daniella."

"No, you're right," Megan said on a sigh. "Nor a Gabrielle. We better get away from the French names and come up with a good old American one. Let's see," she paused, pursing her own lips and narrowing her eyes in concentration, much as Mort had done earlier. "Maybe Leona, for your grandfather Leon?"

"Nope, he never liked his name, and neither do I," Mort replied. "Perhaps Josephine, after your dad, Joseph?"

"Uh-uh," Megan answered, a head shake added for emphasis.

"Maybe after a gem, then. She's our little gem. She could be a Pearl, or an Opal. Or a Ruby. Could even be a zircon or a rhinestone! Come to think of it, Zircon sounds like one of those modern old-fashioned names all the movie stars are naming their kids."

"Now you're being silly," Megan said. "But, you may be on the right track. Is there a flower name we might like? After all, she's not only our little gem: she's our little rose – with her little pouty rosebud mouth."

"Sure, Rose would be great. But Carnation is even better. It might turn out to be *the* name for the daughters of the new decade," Mort deadpanned. "Oh – or even better than that – Hollyhock!"

By now Megan had begun to giggle. "Mort, you are so goofy. It's a shame we can't name her after you."

"Or after you," Mort replied. His eyes widened and his eyebrows rose to his hairline. Megan could tell he was getting a brand new idea, practically seeing the idea form inside his head. "We could name her Megan."

Megan smiled, looking at her husband with love in her eyes. "Oh, Mort, that is so lovely of you to even think of naming her after me." She gingerly sat up higher in her bed, rearranging the baby against her bosom. And she, too, was thinking. "What if we put our two names together, Mort and Megan? We could perhaps name her Morgan. How does that sound?

"Morgan Freeman," Mort said, trying the name out on his tongue. It seemed to roll off nicely. He repeated, "Morgan Freeman." He turned to Megan and hugged her, trying hard to neither dislodge the baby nor to hurt Megan in the process. "Morgan and Freeman sound good together, but boy, does that sound familiar for some reason. Does it sound familiar to you?

"Yeah, it does, but I can't place it. Oh, well, it sounds good; we like it; it's a pretty name; so let's go with it. Maybe use my middle name Anne with it?"

"Okay, it's a done deal. Morgan Anne Freeman, it is!" Then Megan heard him repeat "Morgan Freeman" under his breath several times, just getting a feel for the way the names formed in his mouth.

The baby was now sleeping against Megan's shoulder so Mort helped her move over slightly, allowing him space on the hospital bed. He climbed in and pressed as closely to Megan as possible.

"Let's watch a little TV. I know they gave you some medicine to relax you. Perhaps the background noise will lull you and maybe you can get a nap while Morgan is asleep."

Megan yawned and nodded gratefully. She turned her cheek into Mort's neck, sighing peacefully as she settled against him.

He turned on the TV with the remote control and ran through the channels. Loud cops and robbers shows, bull riding, laugh-track filled sit-coms, and rap music appeared to be his choices. He searched for a movie that might be low-key and with soothing elevator type music. He found "Driving Miss Daisy" and settled in to watch. Megan gently snored by his side.

Suddenly he sat straight up and excitedly yelled, "There's Morgan Freeman!"

"What?" Megan asked, struggling up from her drugged sleep. Morgan began to fret and to cry that pitiful newborn squeak.

More quietly Mort said, "Look Megan. There's Morgan Freeman! That's who our daughter is named after."

Megan peered at the TV screen and brought her hand up to her mouth to stifle her laugh while also trying to pat Morgan's back. She watched Morgan Freeman, the tall, dignified black actor, as he slowly drove along the tree-lined street with his employer, Miss Daisy, serenely riding in the back seat. "Yes ma'am, Miss Daisy," he courteously said, a small smile of affection playing around his mouth.

Mort and Megan looked at each other and each smiled in contentment and satisfaction. Their Morgan was well named. Each had his own thoughts about the name. Wouldn't it be a hoot if she were to grow up and be a competing name in Hollywood, Mort thought. Maybe the competition wouldn't last too long, since the current Morgan Freeman of Hollywood fame was getting along in years.

Megan, musing, could see her child's name up on a theatre marquee, announcing some exciting new film "Starring Morgan Freeman." Her name in lights! Oh, how splendid that would be!

A picture of their lovely daughter would have to accompany it, of course. There must be *no* confusion about just who she is. She is their little star. Hers and Mort's. Morgan.

IT'S ALL ABOUT PERSPECTIVE

J AN AND I forged an unlikely
relationship. One forced on us by
our husbands. They were US Marines, helicopter pilots, sent to Afghanistan
to participate in the war on terror. They met in flight school and instantly
became buddies. Jan and I met several times at social events, but hadn't really
clicked. But when our men were preparing to go to war, they thought it to be
a brilliant idea for the two wives to share accommodations and costs while
attending the university, Jan to continue work on her undergraduate degree,
and I to enroll in a Master's program in Education. We agreed to move in
together, and here we were in our second month of living together.

The day I drove my husband to the airport to leave for war, I was beset
with loneliness and devastated at the thought of a year, or more, without
him. My devastation was quite complete upon my entry into the apartment
I was sharing with Jan and my discovery that she had systematically divided
everything into halves. The refrigerator had all her items on one side; each
shelf from top to bottom held her jars of condiments, sandwich makings,
milk, and other food necessities. The other half was pristinely empty,

awaiting, as Jan said, my things, which we would keep separate from hers because we obviously cooked and ate differently. I was slightly offended, since this seemed to be a slam against my Southern cooking and womanly figure. Hers ran more to the "Twiggy" look, and her cooking ran more to opening a yogurt and slicing a piece of cheese.

I found, too, that the linen closet was neatly aligned to the left with her towels and sheets, a shelf for each, plus storage for blankets and assorted items. I rightly assumed my side was the right half, currently empty. I sighed, wondering how I would survive this year with such a strange woman but, against everything my gut was saying to me, I thanked her for being so thoughtful and neat.

Now I'm in our apartment complex pool, lazily stroking aside the cool, clear water and forcing myself to relax. I try to empty my head of the school projects that are piling up like firewood stacked beside the fireplace on a snowy night. Then I hear it. It's growing louder. A mewling sound of hurt – or deep pain. Slinging the tendrils of wet hair out of my eyes with a jerking twist of my head, I look to the poolside.

Something is clearly wrong. The face Jan wears is crumpled, her lips wide in a wail and her eyes pulled together in the middle of her face by the deep ruts that sprang up between her eyebrows. Her forehead is creased deeply with wrinkles. She, who never frowns for fear of marring her beauty. And her eyes are strange. They're dripping tears, but seem wild and unfocused. What could possibly have put her into such a state?

Then I see it. She is frantically waving a small square of white paper in her hand as she works her throat, trying to speak. Through her gasps and hitching breath, she can only say one word. My name. "Lily." It comes out on a shuddering sob. Adrenalin hits in a rush. Scrambling from the pool, I stand dripping at the top of the ladder in front of her.

"Jan, what on Earth is the matter? What's the problem? Why are you crying?"

Again waving the paper at me, she continues sobbing, her entire body jerking as I reach out to hold her shoulders. She moves in a spasmodic dance, putting one foot down, then the other, then lifting one and repeating the motions, quickly, over and over. She literally can't be still.

I take the paper from her jerking hand, the ink smearing as the water from my hand and fingers transmogrify it into a spreading stain that makes the printing on it barely legible. I narrow my eyes and peer through the slim slits and I can just make out the letters. They aren't letters at all, but two phone numbers in running blue ink. I turn the card over and the reverse side reads: Captain George Donnelly, Chaplain, USMC.

A brilliant light turns on in my head and dread of the stomach-sinking variety begins blooming in my gut.

"It's Johnny, isn't it?" I ask with other-worldly calm.

Jan is still doing her frenetic dance and is now wringing her hands. "Ye-e-ess," she wails, drawing out the word in her agony. "He's dead, Lily. He's dead!"

With my still dripping body supporting her, and my slick, wet arm around her back and shoulder, I murmur inane, nonsensical, but comforting words to her, speaking softly, low and soothingly, as I begin to steer her back to the second floor apartment we share in this sprawling, mostly student, complex. Behind my crooning, my thoughts are flying in all directions, like wild birds caught in a cage.

I had been in the pool for only a few minutes when Jan broke my reverie. The Chaplain and the USMC military policeman must have been coming up one set of stairs to the apartment while I was going down another. A part of me is wishing I had been there to offer support to Jan when the news came to her. Another part of me is supremely grateful that I had not been in the apartment when the two men came to call.

All military wives, especially those whose husbands are in a combat zone, fear that knock on the door and the two men standing there in uniform.

Young military officers don't make a lot of money, and for those wives, like Jan and me, who are going back for college degrees and not presently employed, it is a necessity to room together. At our last wives get-together before our husbands were flown away to Afghanistan, we couldn't help but talk about the "what-if's." It was talked about, and was candidly agreed upon by all of us, that if we are rooming with another wife, and if one of us opens the door to see the two uniformed men (as a military policeman always accompanies the chaplain, whose job it is to break the bad news and offer comfort and condolences), we would unashamedly hope that they were there for the other wife and not for one's self.

That would have been the case had I opened that door a few minutes ago instead of Jan. I am truly sorry for her loss, but deeply relieved it was she, and not I, who had received the news.

Once inside, I sit Jan down on the end of the couch and hurry to heat some hot chocolate. She needs to have something soothing to help her stop shaking. She is neither a coffee nor hot tea drinker, so I fervently hope the chocolate will do the trick. Continuing to talk soothingly to her, I get out the milk and Nestle Quick and add them to the pan. Once I place the mug of hot cocoa in her hand, she wraps both hands around it and takes a couple of tentative sips. That calms her a bit. She swallows a few more sips and then asks, "What do I do now?"

"I think perhaps you should call your mom and dad. And Johnny's parents. They all need to know, and they can help you make decisions on what to do next." I get her address book from her room and bring it to her.

"Jan, I'll make any calls you want me to. Just tell me who. I suppose the numbers are all in here?" I ask, taking the book back and holding it open in my hands.

"Yes. But, I'm going to call my mom and dad right now. Oh," she doubles over in a fresh wave of pain, "I can't believe it. I can't believe Johnny's gone."

"Jan, let me call your folks. When I get them on the line you can talk to them. Okay?"

"Okay," she agrees, sniffing and wiping the tears from her face onto the back of her hand.

I punch in the digits as she gives them to me. A woman's bright voice answers, "Hello?"

"Mrs. Harding, this is Lily, Jan's roommate," I say, not giving her a chance to exchange pleasantries. "Jan wants to talk to you." I hand the phone to Jan and watch her face crumple again as a fresh set of tears appear upon just hearing her mother's voice.

She musters enough control to relay the information to her mother. In her doing so, I hear for the first time exactly what had happened and how Johnny had died. "They told me his helicopter flew into a mountain. It crashed to the ground and everybody on board was killed instantly." She breaks down again, sobbing. Struggling to speak, she continues, "Oh, Mom, I still can't believe it. It doesn't seem real."

I go to her and hold her hand. "Can you finish, Jan? Or do you want me to talk to your mom?"

"No. I'll be all right. Thanks," she says, without attempting to pull free her hand.

I let go her hand and pat it as I sit down beside her on the couch. Well, now I know what the cause of death is. I am feeling so bad for Jan, but my heart is bleeding for the devastating loss of Johnny and his crew.

Jan finishes her call to her mom and then takes several long, slow, deep breaths. "Okay, I'm ready to call Mr. and Mrs. Williams." We had been taught to do that exercise to help relieve stress and calm down at one of our Officer's Wives Club functions. Now, the practice is coming in handy, since it really does seem to help Susan regain some measure of control.

She speaks to Johnny's mom, who immediately screams for her husband upon learning of Johnny's death. His father then talks with Jan at some length, requesting the phone numbers from the ink-stained card. I read them off to her while she repeats them to him. Her voice is a little stronger now that someone will relieve her of the burden of having to make all the plans. Mr. Williams says that he'll see that Johnny's body is brought home for burial in the nearby National Cemetery.

Now that she's done with that call, I suggest, "Okay, Honey, I think you need some rest. Your whole system has had a dreadful shock." I fall back on my natural Southern terms of comfort. Normally, I could never feel free calling her "Honey," because she wouldn't appreciate the familiarity.

"I can't rest. There's too much to do."

"Let his parents and the Marine Corps handle it now. Tell you what: I'll give you half of one of my sleeping pills. They're only herbal and there's nothing in them that can harm you, and I really think the rest, and the sleep, just to get your mind off this for a while, will do you a world of good."

Although it is nowhere near bedtime, Jan looks at the darkening sky out our window and sighs. "I guess you're right, Lily. Okay, I'll take a half."

I get one of my tablets and cut it in half. I offer it to her with a glass of water at her bedside. Usually meticulously neat, she pulls off her clothes and lays them on her desk chair. Even so, it is a deviation from her normal habit of hanging everything neatly in her closet or laying them carefully folded in her drawer. She slips on a nightgown while I turn down her bed. She sits on the side of it and downs the pill with a few sips of water.

"Should I close the door?" I ask as I'm leaving the room.

"No, please leave it open. I don't want to be alone."

"Okay, then. I'll be right out here if you need me."

I hear her sobbing for a while, and then the unaccustomed pill kicks in and she goes to sleep, curled on her side in the fetal position, as if trying to protect her heart with her drawn up knees.

The next day her parents come. They pack up all her things and take her and her possessions home with them. They go by the university on their way and check her out of school. She will enroll at the university in her home town and begin a new life there.

That night I receive a call from my husband. He wants me to know Johnny's death is due to a freak accident and he sure as hell does not intend for it to happen to him. Before ending our call, I tell him I plan to drive to Johnny's home town so that I can be there for the military funeral. He cautions me that the funeral will be a very tough one to get through and that perhaps I should take a friend with me for emotional support.

I do. I ask a very old friend who has met Jan to go with me and we take several hours, driving along the Gulf coast, getting out and walking shoeless on the glowing white sandy beach, feeling the aqua waters rushing to meet our toes. We almost forget why we're here and where we're going.

At the funeral, Jan looks regal and sorrowful, a true vision of loveliness in her slim black dress. She, as do I, jumps every time the volley of shots rings out. While *Taps* is playing, my tears drip like rain water onto the program I hold in my hands.

I say goodbye to Jan and we utter the usual niceties about keeping in touch, each of us knowing we will not. We are two people thrown together by chance and separated by fate. Inordinately different, we never truly bonded. But I was the person she did have when she needed someone, so it was to me that she came that day. The day that changed her life, and in doing so, changed mine.

I find a new roommate. I think about what could have been with Susan and me, but simply wasn't. I continually find it with my new roommate. She is a grad student like me, but not a military wife. And she is the one who finds me at the pool and tells me some Marine officers are waiting to see me. She is the one comforting me in my devastation at the senseless loss of my husband to a roadside bomb in an unpopular war. We are true friends and she, unlike Jan, is a part of my life and will be always.

JUST ANOTHER SECRET

I'M PREPARING COQ au vin for dinner. I chop the onion and slice the mushrooms and gather all the ingredients to brown the chicken.

My daughter, Nikki, enters the periphery of my vision. She is a junior in high school, a good daughter, a good student, and quite mature and independent for her age. One look at her frowning face tells me something is wrong.

"What's up, Nikki?"

"Nothing." A deep sigh follows.

"Nothing?"

"Not really."

"Why don't you tell me about it and we'll see if it's anything?" I say.

"Well, um, all right."

"So?" I prompt.

"Mom, you remember the hundred dollar bill I had?"

Had? "Yes, did something happen to it?"

"Kind of. Remember, I went to the movie with Tracy the other afternoon?"

"Ri-ii-i-ight." I slowly say, as I look at her and await an explanation.

"Well, I'd laid the hundred dollar bill in the top of my purse. I must have knocked it out when I got money for popcorn, because later I couldn't find it."

"Are you sure? Did you check all around the seat and everywhere?"

"Yes, of course, I did."

"Okay, get the phone number for the theatre and we'll call and ask if anyone turned it in. Fat chance of that, I'm sure, but it's worth a try."

"I've already done that, Mom. I asked the manager then to let me know if anyone turns it in. He said he would call me if they did. He didn't call, so I just checked with them again to see if they had it and he said no one turned it in and the cleaning crew didn't find it. I guess it is lost for good." She winds down this outburst.

"I'm sorry, honey, but I think you've learned a valuable lesson here. It was irresponsible to just lay it in the top of your purse that way. Hundred dollar bills are hard to come by. I know you worked hard baby-sitting to earn that money. What possessed you to change it all into one bill, anyway?"

"I thought it would be safer if I had only one bill to deal with."

"Perhaps, but you should never have carried it with you. It belonged in the bank, or at least you needed to leave it at home so it couldn't get lost," I lecture freely.

"I know."

"Well, it's done with now. Nothing we can do about it. So just count it as a loss and start building your savings account all over again."

"Yes ma'am, I will."

A couple of days later I climb the stairs and start down the hall to my room, treading on the heavily padded carpet and making no sound. I hear Nikki on the phone in her room talking to Tracy. She is asking how Tracy is feeling. I didn't know anything was wrong with Tracy so I, thinking nothing of it, stop to listen to the conversation about how Tracy is doing. I'm not hiding. Nikki can look out her door and see me at any time.

My ears perk up and my heart pounds as I hear Nikki ask, "So you aren't sore or anything after the abortion? They just sucked it out and that was that?"

There is a pause while Tracy fills her in and then Nikki says, "I told my Mom I lost the hundred dollars at the movie. You don't have to worry about paying me back any time soon. This will be our secret."

While Tracy obviously tells her about what happened and what's now going on, I continue to my room. My head is spinning and my stomach is nauseous just thinking about the whole situation Tracy has found herself in and the lies told to cover it up. I'm equally as sick over Nikki's duplicity. I wonder if I should talk to Tracy's Mom. My head hurts with all the thoughts racing through it. And, if I did speak with her mom, I'd have to tell Nikki I had overheard her conversation. On the plus side, in the past, Nikki has never been able to keep a secret from me. She simply loves to share things with me and usually hurries home from school to spill the latest gossip and the activities of everyone she knows. I figure it won't be long before she tells me this one. I decide to wait.

Two days later I am in the kitchen preparing dinner, tearing the lettuce and slicing the vegetables for the salad, when she arrives home from school.

"Mom, I need to tell you something," she abruptly announces.

My pulse races. "Okay."

"Oh, Mom . . . ." She's clearly agitated. "I didn't want to tell you. Remember the hundred dollars I lost?" At my nod, she continues, "Well, I didn't lose it. I gave it to Tracy for an abortion."

"I see," I say steadily. "Don't you think you and I, and Tracy and her mom, should talk about this?"

"Oh Mom, I don't want to do that. I promised I'd keep it a secret." She sighs deeply and continues, "But I know you're right."

With every outward expression yelling "NO," Nikki turns to me and bravely says, "Let's go. Let's do it now before I feel like a traitor for reneging on my promise."

Her hand in mine, we set off down the street, trepidation galloping in my heart as loudly as betrayal sings in hers.

BUTTERFLIES AND RAP MUSIC

Dissociative Identity Disorder. D.I.D. What used to be called Multiple Personalities. Be able to deal with seven, twelve, twenty-three, or even more separate personalities? I'd say, "No way!" But when the person who is a host body for a whole bunch of different, distinct personalities is someone you love, then you have to deal with it.

Deal with it I do. Never because I either want to or have to, but because I need to. There's a difference. *Wanting* to would mean I have an eager desire to make it be all right. To fix it. Or at least to go with it as it is. *Having* to would mean I had no control over doing it at all and simply had to do it, no argument allowed. *Needing* to meant I had to be alert at all times, wary at all hours, ready – at the turn of a word or an expression – to change myself in preparation for whatever. To go on defense, go into protective mode, or do damage control. You see, the person whose body contains nineteen people is my sister Emma.

Our mother is a grade B, well – maybe a grade C, movie and TV star. Work is steady for her, but she's got one of those faces you always recognize but you can't recall her name. You wake up in the middle of the night and go, "Anita!" That's right; Anita is her name. At least it's her stage name. Her real name is Matilda. She's in the limelight often enough that her daughter's strange and often embarrassing behavior could be fodder for the Hollywood gossip rags if the paparazzi did their jobs. Worst case scenario – Emma could switch personalities at any time while they were out in the adoring public. And Anita would . . . well, Anita wouldn't use it to her benefit for publicity by, let's say, recognizing the illness, admitting her child had it, and perhaps being a spokesperson for it. No, Anita wouldn't do that. Anita would be horribly embarrassed, as if having a child with such a problem would make her star shine less brightly and make her either an object of pity or, God forbid, a laughing stock.

Anita did her part to keep the embarrassment at bay by enrolling Emma, and me, in a Protestant Academy for our high school years. It is a school where oral prayer and silent classes alternate throughout the school day. After school we were met at the school's front door by Mother's driver and taken home. Whenever and where ever, I was witness to the switching and had to interact with whichever of the selves came forward at the time. This way, my mother's conscience was clear; she had provided Emma with a playmate, a confidant, a companion. What she did, whether she was actually aware of it or not, was to effectively rid me of a childhood and to stifle my social life as a teen.

Our father is a businessman and works for a company that keeps him on the road most of the time. It's A-Okay with him because he doesn't have to be involved with the upbringing of his kids. We have a home in the hills just off Los Feliz Boulevard in Los Angeles. A few blocks away from us is where the big movie stars live. Some of my favorite TV stars like Katherine Heigle and Ellen Pompeo live real close to me and I see them a lot. They're real cool. And Griffith Park is close.

Now, going to Griffith Park should be a fun activity for two younger teen girls, but it was a real challenge for me when Emma and I went together because she often switched identities at least once during each outing. There were some real surprises and also some really embarrassing moments. Occasionally a care-giving personality came forward and oversaw the conversation and actions so that Emma didn't make a complete idiot of both herself and me. It was trying, to say the least, and if I hadn't loved my vulnerable and sweet sister Emma, I'd have been so out of there long before I could legally do so.

Emma is two years older than I but it has always seemed that I was the older. I suppose the responsibilities you've got to assume when you're barely old enough to know who *you* are, much less who that strange voice coming from your fifteen year old sister is, will make you grow up in a hurry.

I don't know just when the D.I.D. started with Emma. Mother and Father thought she was being rude or purposefully disobeying them when totally unaccustomed behavior emerged. I thought she was just acting like a weirdo.

Even I, however, realized something was clearly wrong when we were at Griffith Park one afternoon in late spring. We rode the merry-go-round first thing like we've always done and then decided we would go to the concession stand for a coke. As we headed for the concessions, Emma started jabbering like a baby – at least like she was about three years old.

I said, "Hey, Emma! What are you carrying on about?" She just continued to talk like a little kid about the butterflies fluttering around. She *sounded* like some little kid I didn't even know! And when she asked the man at the drinks cart for a coke, she leaned forward on her elbows on the top of the cart with her chin in her hands and wiggled her rear from side to side. To top it off, she couldn't seem to make up her mind about what she wanted, when I knew she came for a coke. In this real babyish voice she finally asked for an orange drink. Whoa! Something was definitely wrong with that. Emma hated orange drink!

"Thank you, Mister," she told him, just like we were taught to do when we were little. But we weren't little! So what in the devil was wrong with her, anyway?

"Emma, cut it out! You're being stupid."

She looked at me with these wide, sincere eyes. "My name is Jenny."

Talk about blow me away – it was like I'd been knocked over by a tornado. "What?"

"I'm Jenny. Emma's not here right now," she said in that same baby voice.

Okay, even at thirteen years old, I knew something was wrong. But I just put it down to Emma being goofy. I couldn't imagine anything else. We started walking back to where the driver was to pick us up and Emma remarked in her own voice that she hoped he'd be on time because she had a project she wanted to finish that afternoon.

"What happened to Jenny?"

"Who's Jenny?"

"You just said your name was Jenny!"

She looked at me like I'd gone crazy and said in this real huffy voice that really belonged to her, "What are you talking about, Susie? You are so stupid sometimes!"

I knew arguing with her was pointless so I just clammed up. I did wonder about her, however. Jenny? Who the crap was Jenny?

After that first time when I was aware that someone else's voice entirely was coming from Emma and that the voice and actions matched that of a young child, there were many more to follow. Sometimes it was Jenny. Other times it was Monique. Monique was fun. I have to admit that I really liked Monique because she was sixteen, not four like I found Jenny to be, and she loved to dance wildly to the latest rap songs, making up her own naughty lyrics. After Monique left and I was brought back to my senses with Emma, I wondered how and where Emma had learned the outrageous things that Monique said and did.

Then there was Ralph, a boy! Ralph was thirteen and he was a regular juvenile delinquent. He had a rebellious dark side and was always planning how he could run away. He also liked to flirt with me. I knew when Ralph was there because Emma's voice became deeper and her whole demeanor changed to that of a moody young teen boy. He could be fun, especially when he was either flirting with me or picking on me.

I tried to protect Emma by keeping her away from Mother and Father as much as possible so they couldn't see just how many people lived inside her. I knew by the time she was seventeen and I was fifteen, two years after I first truly knew about Jenny, that she was gaining more and more identities and switching more often. But they knew. I overheard them talking about it even before the decision was made to send us to the private school. They asked that I take a special test to see if I might skip a grade, thus allowing me to be in the same grade as Emma. She'd goofed off and flunked one grade a couple of years back. I'd always made excellent grades and was at the top of my classes. So, I passed the test and we entered the Protestant Academy when we were both going into the tenth grade. It was a small elite school and so Emma and I were in the same classes. Her caretaker self, Marcia, would come out and see to Emma's behavior, keeping quiet Monique, Ralph, Jenny, and by now, several others.

Sometimes Marcia would be unable to keep a switch from occurring and then the teachers and the other students would stare or laugh at the inappropriate things Emma said and did. Finally this was discussed by all the staff and the principal called Mother and Father in for a conference. The upshot was that they would have to get counseling for Emma. Of course, we didn't know then what we would find out. And the powers that be in the school surely didn't have a clue. We did discover that there were studies where all the individual identities could be integrated back into just one person.

Emma began seeing a counselor who specialized in this field. We found out that it was highly unusual for someone as young as Emma to exhibit the signs of DID. She always has to be different!

It took a long time during our three high school years and throughout four years of college for it to be moderately successful. The identities knew about each other and they could also talk to each other. Through hypnosis, the counselor put Emma in a sleep-like state and found out about each one. Sometimes there was deep anger, or even violence, on some identity's part, directed at Emma. Some parts thought they were the main one and Emma was just another of the identities. If Sam, an eighteen year old boy-man, came out, he'd often try to harm Emma.

I sometimes drove around our neighborhood and out to Griffith Park, but never did I drive on the freeways like the Five or one of the bigger roads. Drive along Los Feliz, or down Hillhurst, or Sunset or Wilshire, I would do, even though I had no driver's license and Anita would be at her most dramatic angriest if she should find out. I would sneak Anita's little red Mazda sports car when she was off doing a movie shoot and Emma and I would have a blast. Mother would also have an academy award winning tantrum if she knew Emma and I referred to her as Anita.

One afternoon after Mother's driver took Emma to counseling, I was snooping in the gowns and sequined dresses in Mother's closet when I got a cell phone call from Emma. She had just found in her latest journal in which she wrote her thoughts, and in which the other parts could write theirs, a note from Sam saying she'd better watch out because he meant to do her serious harm. It was written in blood.

Practically scared to death and crying uncontrollably, she begged me to come get her. She was too afraid to go inside to counseling for fear Sam would come out and, indeed, get her. The hand writing was most certainly not Emma's, but she recognized it to be Sam's from when he'd come out before and had written threatening notes to her.

In the Mazda, I flew down Los Feliz, careened onto Vermont, and skidded to a stop in the counselor's parking lot on Franklin. I have no idea if I even saw a traffic signal, much less if I obeyed it. I threw open the door and rushed to Emma who was standing inside crying her eyes out. She flung her arms around me and clung to me as if I was literally saving her life. I was so busted! Now, I had to tell Anita I'd driven her car and why.

We found a different counselor – one who was able to keep Sam a little more subdued when he appeared, and who through daily sessions was also able to start integrating the now nineteen distinct identities. Our high school years were grueling. I hardly made it with my sanity intact. And Emma? I've never known anyone to put her whole self into someone's hands and work that body, and mind, to the breaking point with therapy sessions every weekday.

The following years at the small Protestant college were sometimes calm, sometimes not. Sam continued to threaten. Ralph continued to flirt with me, even though I had long passed his age of thirteen. Marcia still reigned as the mother figure for all.

The counselor, nearing the end of our senior year and graduation from "Churchy U," as we called it, felt the parts had been integrated back into just Emma. Under hypnosis, Emma revealed the yardman in our neighborhood, gone now, had sexually abused her several times when she was four. She needed to escape, to go somewhere else while he did that, so she invented the personalities who later multiplied.

A confident, smiling Emma strode across the stage to receive her graduation diploma. I watched her from my seat on stage as the Valedictorian. The press was there, alerted no doubt by Anita. Great Photo Op.

We continued to live with Anita and Dad after graduation from college. I got a job as a school teacher at the nearby Montessori school where I

could teach kids who already gave me a run for my money. And I thought
I was smart!

Emma is shy by nature so she was delighted to secure a position as a
pre-school teacher at our Protestant Academy, where she daily saw the
same teachers we had in high school. She felt safe from any recurrence
of the D.I.D. She was integrated, all identities combined again into just
Emma.

But, every now and then, Emma finds herself wearing something she has
no recollection of buying, or eating something she didn't order. So – who
did?

OUR NIGHTMARISH NEIGHBOR

"**H**EY, DID YOU hear we're going to get a new neighbor?" Martha called down the hall to her neighbor and good friend, Betty.

"Why no," Betty replied, wiping the sweat from her brow with her billowing exercise shirt. Some people exercised in these cute little form-fitting outfits that showed off everything they had under them. That was most definitely not what Betty wore to exercise. If it should emphasize her curves, or worst of all, should it cling to her ample bosom, then she was scandalized. Not just for herself, but for the ogling party as well. On this day, garbed in flowing shirt and loose shorts, she had attended her dratted exercise class, which she hated with every fiber of her being. Doctor's orders.

Exercise classes were just one of the benefits Betty and Martha shared with the other residents who lived in their retirement community, one of the most desirable and most well-appointed in the city. Drawing inspiration from the ancient oak trees with their long, grey beards of trailing Spanish moss, the developers named the community Majestic Oaks.

That was quite a lovely and lofty name for a retirement community, they both thought, but kept this notion to themselves for fear of irritating some old person (yes, there were many who were older than the two friends) and causing a ruckus. It was true, however. Majestic Oaks was a lovely place to live. Set on the grounds of a former plant nursery, it was gorgeous, to say the least. Red knockout roses could be found all over the campus with their scarlet nimbus of tightly furled or full-blown blooms. The gardeners dead-headed weekly, before any fading blooms could mar their beauty.

The grounds boasted azaleas pouring forth a perfect profusion of pink flowers in the spring. Due to the unusually warm weather they had been having for the last couple of years, the azalea blooms were bursting forth in early December, as well. It must be terribly confusing for a plant, Martha thought, with them never knowing when they would bloom. Additionally, every kind of camellia could be found almost anywhere on the property, their blooms varied, their colors ranging from white to deepest vermillion with every shade in-between. Yes, it was a lovely place to live for so many interesting reasons.

And now they were to have a new neighbor in the empty apartment at the end of the hall. It had sat empty for several months since their long-time friend, Ann, had moved to the area of the campus known as Assisted Living. The two friends knew that would be their fate one day, but for now they were happy where they were – right here in this three story apartment building, and on the third floor, at that.

Three days later, the rumors became reality when a moving van pulled up out front of the apartment building with the four moving men hurriedly climbing down from the cab (they must have been packed like sardines in there, Martha thought) and quickly raising the back door of the van. That gave the nosy twosome a bird's eye view of its contents from their perch on the third floor screened porch.

Black. Black. And more black. A black sofa and two black overstuffed parlor chairs from what must have been the late 1800's. Black velvet paintings of weird stuff, some of which looked an awful lot like Yvonne DeCarlo, who played Lily Munster on TV, way back in the 1960's. Black clothing was visible as the shapeless pieces hung from the huge hands of the moving men.

There wasn't too much in the way of kitchen goods. No dish packs, no big boxes of pots and pans. They didn't see anything that looked like bedroom furniture. There were two trunks like the old steamer trunks of many years ago, painted black, of course.

Martha and Betty turned to each other, their eyes wide and their mouths gaping.

"Are you seeing what I'm seeing?" Martha bleated to Betty.

"I don't understand that taste at all. Must all be in the mouth," Betty replied.

It was at that moment that the new neighbor emerged from the impressive vintage car, a black Cadillac that followed the van and had to have been from the 1960's as well. No, make that the late '50's, maybe a '58, when all the cars were recognizable by year.

"She *does* look like Lily Munster!" Betty shrieked.

"Hush, she'll hear you!" Martha cautioned.

Too late. Both of them ducked as the lady of whom they spoke looked up – and looked directly at them. Her dark eyes gleamed with what might possibly be amusement. They each fervently hoped it was amusement. She was just too frightening for words. She had long black hair that hung down below her shoulders, a white face, and was thin to the point of emaciation.

"She definitely could use a haircut," Betty chose to say at that moment, breaking some of the tension in the air.

"And some modern clothes," Martha added. "My Lord, that black, droopy stuff went out with the Hippies in the '60's." If the look she cast sideways at Betty's outfit had any hidden meaning, Betty chose to ignore it.

They turned their attention back to the movers who were at this moment wrestling with a very long, fairly narrow, cardboard box that appeared to be immensely heavy.

"Why, that looks like a box a big couch would come in," Betty said.

"Or a coffin!"

They gave each other looks of horror and then each strode rapidly away to her own door and the safety their apartments provided. They were definitely uneasy.

The new neighbor finished moving in, thanks to the four muscle-bound movers who had their work cut out for them in hauling that big box to the third floor. She seldom was seen, although by now all the building's tenants were on the lookout for her. When she did emerge from her apartment, it always seemed to be at night. Once, when Martha asked her if she liked to go out to eat in the evening, the new neighbor's reply was but one word, "Yes." This was accompanied by a curving smile that exposed some teeth in need of capping. Martha couldn't help but notice that she did have unusually long canine teeth, or eye teeth, as they were called when Martha was young.

Soon after the arrival of the new neighbor, the plants and flowers on the campus of the retirement community began to fade. Some drooped, even though they were watered frequently. Some lost their blooms even though the head gardener applied more fertilizer. In no time they were all turning black with slick, slimy branches which oozed black goop. Should anyone come too close to one of the once lovely knockout roses, it seemed that the bush's branches reached out to leave a deep thorn prick in an arm, a leg, a hand, or a foot. The smaller flowers in the beautiful beds simply shriveled and died.

And now there were new, and quite disturbing, incidences of accidental deaths in the surrounding neighborhoods located near Majestic Oaks. The coroner said, that in each case, the victim had an accident whereby one or more major arteries had either been severed or punctured so deeply until the victim exsanguinated.

"What? All their blood was gone? It just ran out of them?" Betty asked at their meeting of concerned citizens.

"Yeah, and if it did, where did it go?" Martha backed her up.

There were no satisfactory answers to the dilemma. Everyone was confused, except maybe the lone figure in the back of the room who sat with legs and arms crossed, wearing all black, and assessed the complainers with glittering eyes.

Not only the people in the new neighbor's apartment building, but everyone who had at some point on some night encountered her strolling along the paths of the grounds, was literally scared to death of her. By now the word on everyone's lips was "Vampire."

Martha and Betty called together their friends from their apartment building, and any other interested souls from the other resident buildings, and decided to right the wrong that they saw happening in their midst by writing a petition. The policies at Majestic Oaks Retirement Community were much the same as at any other. Should there be enough names signed on any petition within normal bounds, the owners, directors, and administration would have to seriously address the complaint and petition.

The petition stated that either the occupant of apartment 309, the newest neighbor, allow the administration to enter her apartment to search for something sinister, or otherwise harmful, or the tenant would have to vacate the apartment and leave the grounds of Majestic oaks.

Our new neighbor shrieked with laughter upon the petition with every resident's name signed on it being presented to her by the Director, with Martha and Betty in his tow.

"I'm sorry, my Sweeties, but you will *never* enter my apartment!" she vowed. She sobered quickly and added, "I certainly don't want to stay where such petty and narrow minded people live, so I shall be on my way tomorrow. It's been anything but pleasant here. I'll be glad to go." She stepped back and closed her door firmly. But before it shut, they could see in the gloom by the moonlight shining through the wide slit in the heavily curtained window that there was indeed a coffin shape in the living room.

The next morning, Martha and Betty stayed in their apartments until the same four movers had her loaded up and she was ready to enter her long black Cadillac and back it out of the parking space. They then emerged, having coordinated their movements by phone, to see her leave.

"We did good on this one, didn't we, Betty? By forcing her out, I mean."

"Absolutely, Martha," Betty said. She grinned, and with the customary twinkle in the eye returning, she added, "I'm the only one around here allowed to wear black, loose fitting clothes! Who'd she think she was, anyhow? A vampire?"

They both shuddered. "I think I felt a cat walk over my grave," Martha said, gathering her light sweater around her on this warm night when the thermometer in this outside hall pointed to 89 degrees.

THE METHODIST CHURCHYARD

IT HAS SURPASSED the test of time. It still waits here, daily anticipating the footsteps of laughing children, the rough voices of the sports coaches, the soft tones of the Sunday School teachers, this Methodist churchyard. For more than a century this churchyard has provided the folk of this tiny town a meeting place for almost anything anyone could think of. I shall relate to you the following stories, which are but a few that this churchyard has witnessed over the years.

*   *   *

The family members stand sobbing quietly as they witness a hanging. A relative, sentenced to die by hanging from the neck from a spreading limb of the aged oak on the neighboring courthouse lawn. His crime was stealing a horse. Depriving one of his horse deprived him of his livelihood in that time of dire poverty. A horse pulled a plow, pulled the family wagon, and carried upon his back the suffering soul who rode near and far in search of a paying job. Retribution was called for.

*   *   *

The churchyard's tin-roof-covered, makeshift picnic tables bear the weight of the hopeless, helpless, and hungry men of the Great Depression. They gather there daily and pray that *this* will be the day that the turpentine mill will need a worker or two, and dare to hope to be chosen. Their stomachs rumble with hunger and their strength ebbs. Meanwhile, they wait.

*   *   *

This churchyard witnesses the frightening, white-robed figures of the Ku Klux Klan, who appear as ghostly apparitions in the flickering firelight. It then sees them ride away on their plow horses to do untold atrocities in the shadow of darkness.

*   *   *

All that was before I arrived on the scene and had my own stories. By my time, the Methodist churchyard is used for more mundane, and certainly happier, occasions. Some are not so happy, however. This is one of those times.

I am barefoot, clothed in ragged shorts held up by a twist of rope around my narrow waist. My soft, faded cotton tee-shirt has an ever-fraying hole above my heart that crawls across my collarbone with every striding step. I follow my big brother Jack across the field behind our house as we make our way to the Methodist churchyard. There he is meeting Bubba, a boy from his class in school, a true bully, and almost twice the size of Jack. They are meeting to fight. It is a matter of honor for Jack. Bubba has made an insulting remark about our mama and that just couldn't be tolerated by a Southern son. Southern boys are known for loving their mamas. And Jack certainly loves our Mama.

I'm not worried. Bubba might be big and scary, but he is a little bit stupid. Anybody who wants to fight Jack is stupid. I know Jack will make him sorry he ever thought, much less said, those insulting words.

Where Jack goes, I go. Since we live almost within spitting distance of the churchyard, we have arrived first. I sit at one of the picnic tables, idly picking at a sandspur thorn I have managed to imbed in the heel of my foot. Jack stands, shoulders back, thin belly sucked in, tanned toes grasping the brittle grass of the churchyard. His dungarees, torn at both knees, seem to want to drag him down, but he stands firm, face turned to the small dirt lane that runs the length of the churchyard, his eyes searching and his ears attuned to the first sound that will indicate Bubba and his gang are near. He lifts his slim, brown hand and casually flicks a ladybug from his bare chest. I grin secretly to myself. Outwardly, Jack is like the calm before the storm, but I know that inside he is a raging tornado.

Bubba and his crew arrive, Jack's eyes following their every move, and begin to hurl insults at him. Jack stands tall, never moving, biding his time until Bubba is near enough to him so it will not seem as if he, Jack, has flown off the handle and has instigated the attack.

Swaggering, his man's khaki work-pants sliding against his heavy thighs, Bubba swiftly approaches the statue that is Jack.

"So," he says, "you're going to try to avenge your low-life daddy, huh? You think you can whip me, boy? Huh? You think you can whip me?"

By now, Bubba has eaten up all the space between them and is within Jack's reach. But, still he stands, unmoving. I know he is waiting for Bubba to throw the first fist. Another insulting yell comes from Bubba, "Why don't you say something? Are you deaf? Are you blind?"

Backing off slightly, and with a puzzled frown furrowing his brow, Bubba yells, "What's the matter with you, anyway?" No response from Jack; just a tight, white line spreading out from his lips, reaching for the jut of his jaw.

Unable to fathom this illogical behavior from his foe, Bubba hauls back his ham-sized hand, clenches the fingers tightly into a fist, and launches it at Jack's face. He has aimed squarely at his nose. I giggled aloud as I watch Bubba's legendary fighting tool arc through the air where but a second before Jack's face had occupied that space.

Jack has ducked to avoid the massive blow Bubba's swing would have landed. Then the tornado is unleashed. Dropping his head, that rightfully should have adorned a Greek God's statue with its curly locks and classical looks, Jack plows straight into Bubba's soft mid-section, its give caused by too many plates of rice and gravy in this time of want.

The force of the counter-attack carries Bubba to the ground where he lies gasping, grunting, and clutching his stomach. In a suspended moment in time, Jack is straddling him.

Watching from my picnic bench perch, it seems as if it is all happening in slow motion. I watch Jack's brown palm open and descend against Bubba's cheek. Once, twice, three times. And yet again. A more demeaning strike could not be imagined. Finished with slapping, Jack balls that slim hand into a tight fist and slams it down into Bubba's nose. Blood erupts, reaching for the sky.

In a deadly calm and quiet voice Jack says, "Take it back." His arm remains cocked, his fist aiming toward Bubba's face. Bubba didn't respond as quickly as perhaps he should, and the white line returns around Jack's mouth, and his fist again slams into Bubba's face, sending up a fresh geyser.

"Okay, okay," Bubba yells. "Just stop it." He flails beneath Jack, who sits firm and clenches his legs to Bubba's sides as if he were riding a horse.

"Okay, what?" Jack asks, leaning over Bubba, both hands holding down Bubba's hands above and on either side of his head. His stare into Bubba's rapidly swelling eyes is terrible to behold.

"Okay, please," Bubba splutters.

Speaking slowly and reasonably, Jack says, "When I let you up, you're going to apologize to me and Lila." I glow with pride to be included. Then a dead calm washes over his face. He lets go Bubba's hands, slides his weight onto one knee and stands up. He stands looking down at the vanquished for a second or so. His fists uncurl and he glances at the skinned knuckles of his right hand. He brings his eyes back to Bubba's where he still lies between his feet. So quietly until I strain to hear, he says, "Don't ever make me fight you again."

He steps away from Bubba, extends a hand to help him up, and puts that now blood-covered hand on his shoulder, turning him in my direction. Jack thrust his hands into the pockets of his old dungarees, dungarees with nothing but holes in the bottoms of the pockets as they had long since lost their sewn seams, and stands with shoulders back and chest out, and watches from hooded eyes as Bubba first looks at him and then at me.

"I'm sorry," he reluctantly says. A frown draws his eyebrows together and turns down the corners of his mouth. "I didn't mean it." It was an apology, but very likely an insincere one.

Jack turns to me where I sit, about ready to burst with pride that he is my brother. "Well, come on, then," he said, holding out that deadly right hand to me. "Let's go."

Bubba slinks over to his buddies and tries to act the big man, but we all know he has been bested. In the next few weeks, Bubba makes a point of cozying up to Jack. I guess he is adhering to the age-old rule: If you can't beat them, join them. Jack tolerates, but does not reciprocate, Bubba's actions.

That next spring Jack celebrates the occasion of his fourteenth birthday with a party at the Methodist churchyard. Yes, Bubba and his crew are there, since most people in town are invited to each other's parties. Jack has gained a new respect from Bubba and his boys and now Bubba wants to be Jack's very best friend. But Jack remembers Bubba's insult, and while he tries to let it go, it still remains, this thought of Bubba insulting our family, buzzing in his head. For today, he puts it aside.

* * *

A Wienie Roast. Today the churchyard witnessed wienies thrust into the fire in the pit, then their consumption as they disappear down the gullets of the large boys who eat with great gusto first one, then another, each slathered deeply with mustard and ketchup. Today the churchyard would witness happiness, celebration, and gluttony of a monstrous scale as the wienies in their buns continue to disappear as quickly as they come from the fire.

* * *

A wedding! It is laudable; the bride in her flowing, ethereal white is a vision of loveliness, and the groom is stiff and hot in his best black winter suit. The soothing strains of "Wither Thou Goest" fade into memory on the warm air of the Methodist church. Outside, the Methodist churchyard shimmers in its radiant glory, far outshining the wedding party. It is springtime and the trees are leafed out, the grass is lush and green, the wisteria perfumes the air purple. The jonquils push their heads from the rain soaked, softly yielding soil, and wave gaily to the naughty dandelions who claim their territory, as if equal to any. This day the churchyard listens to laughter and love floating on the tranquil May air. Resplendent myself in my new yellow dress, I watch the beautiful bride in awe and vow to one day have "Wither Thou Goest" sung at my wedding. Maybe even here in the Methodist Churchyard.

*   *   *

The barbecued chicken smell, the cindery odor wafting about, makes my nose twitch and my mouth salivate. The Methodist churchyard is on this day hosting the Athlete's Banquet for our tiny school. Our athletes garner great praise and so carry deep pride within our chests. My brother Jack is one such. I am another. The churchyard is the site of the banquet tables, placed in long lines end to end, and their accompanying folding metal chairs acting as bold sentries beside each one. In our honor, that of the athletes, the banquet is essentially held in gratitude to the supporters, our families, our friends, those who cheer us on and watch us succeed at our strenuous play. The sports coaches float among us, directing, giving instructions, much like when instructing us in the skills, and the encouragement it takes, to be winners. The churchyard holds our accomplishments as it holds our bodies, with great care and appreciation.

*   *   *

Sometimes disharmony occurs, under the guise of harmony and comradeship. The Methodist churchyard is the site of a political rally. Democrats versus Republicans. A fish-fry is in progress. Tempers flare over fundamental differences, fried mullet, cheese grits and baked beans. Men speak passionately, gesture wildly, and stride across the browning autumn grass of the churchyard. Reason prevails and these mere mortals gaze upon what they have, what they all share, the here and now of this place, this Methodist churchyard. This which belongs equally to all. Our place. Our spot. Our churchyard. I fill my plate and hungrily devour the fish and the soft, salty, buttery grits made by my mama.

*   *   *

Today the children sit, eyes forward, ears attentive to the Sunday School teacher as she imparts to them just one of the many parables of Jesus. She's telling them the story of The Widow's Mite. Beneath their bottoms and cross-legged positions, the Methodist churchyard lies, unfailingly supporting their small bodies. Tiny hands glide out and caress the spiky green tips. Here and there a long spear of grass is pulled and plucked and thoughtlessly placed in a mouth, there to be sucked and chewed effortlessly before being spat out to return limply to its companions.

* * *

Oh, a fieldtrip! Crossing the road from the school, a kindergarten class trips along behind the teacher. The aide traipses behind, gathering up the rear. The trek culminates in story time under one of the ancient oak trees dotting the Methodist churchyard. Soon laughter erupts, children rise, shoes are thrown about at random, and a dozen or more small feet race wetly along the contours of the freshly cut lawn of the Methodist churchyard.

* * *

It serves many purposes, this churchyard. It has witnessed the passing of time immemorial and history unimaginable. It has witnessed both love and hate, joy and sorrow. It has instilled faith, pride and a sense of oneness in those who participate in its offerings. I am infinitely pleased to have had the privilege of witnessing just a miniscule part of it, this history played out in the Methodist churchyard

SURREPTITIOUSLY YOURS

THE MEETINGS BEGAN in the fall when the trees began to bald and to shed their coats, and the aroma of ripening apples perfumed the air. The air, continuously moving on a small current, was a lightweight whirling eddy when compared with the ferocious wind like a nor'easter they could expect later on. For now, for Judith, it was fun to be outside in the crisp air and feel her face turn red and cold. It was heaven for Judith to press her cold cheek against Jose's warm neck and hold it there while he held her tightly against his jacketed chest. These meetings were precious to both of them and they were devastated at the thought of having to give them up. For, give them up, it seemed they must.

In this western corner of Virginia, far away from the hustle and flow of northern Virginia's madness and the academia of the Charlottesville area, one could slow down and enjoy life. Enjoy the simple things in life, such as picking the red, ripe, sweet, cold-skinned apples that grow in abundance in this lower mountain area.

Judith's father owns the apple orchard that Jose has come to pick apples in. Jose is a second generation Mexican American from just north of the US/Mexico border in southern Texas. While he is extremely good looking, smart, and a high school graduate, he must support his family with his father. That's the way it's always been. That's the way his father wants it. And his father, Tito, is boss. He says they will pick apples in Virginia, so they pick apples in Virginia.

Judith's father would never in a million years allow Judith to be see Jose on even an innocent basis, so they must hide. So, here they are, wrapped closely together in the orange and yellow autumn, treasuring this stolen time together, savoring the spicy scent of the apples and the one of a kind scents of each other.

The two young people were immediately attracted to each other upon meeting. They were introduced in this same apple orchard when Judith came home for the weekend from school at James Madison University. One look at the handsome young man her father was introducing her to and she was a goner. Head over heels. It appeared to be the same for Jose. He stammered a response to her enthusiastic and welcoming greeting, all the while trying not to be too forward.

Now, home again, this time on the sly, with no one but Jose knowing she is there, Judith has come for another rendezvous with Jose. She is ready to be Jose's completely. Jose knows he wants only her. But there is something she must tell him. Oh, she *so* does not want to tell him that she is engaged to be married.

The wedding is to be in June of the coming summer. The only thing she can possibly do is to just tell him and hope he will understand. Hope they can both forget each other. For a wild moment, while her emotions wage war, she considers giving up her intended for a life with Jose.

Now, holding her cold cheek against his warm neck, she turns her head and raises her face so that their lips meet. The kiss deepens while their warm, exhaled breath hangs in the frosty air. Judith wrenches her face away and fiercely holds him tighter against her.

"What's wrong, Judith?"

Judith draws in a deep breath and exhales loudly through her nose. "Ohhh, Jose!" She stops, swallows, and continues rapidly before she can chicken out, "I think I'm in love with you and I think you love me, too." She peers into his dark eyes, which are now gleaming at her declaration of love.

"Yes, yes, I love you, too, Judith!" Jose vehemently vows, his voice low and husky with love and desire.

"But wait, Jose. I have something I have to tell you." Her eyes well with tears and she lifts her gloved hand to swipe them away. Jose presses his warm tongue to the cool curve of her cheek and licks away the last sliding tear. Touched by his selfless act of love, Judith's tears breach her lower lids again.

"Why are you crying, Judith? What's wrong?"

Practically strangling on the words, Judith whispers, "I'm engaged to be married next summer."

At Jose's stunned expression, she continues, "But I don't want to marry him now. I love *you!*"

Judith sags with relief as Jose's arms tighten around her, pulling her back into his embrace, warming her with his body. "So, what do we do now, Judith? This is like a fairy tale to me, like where the Black Knight wins the fair maiden from the White Knight. How can we do that? How do we make it work?"

Sniffing back the tears and a now runny nose, Judith offers a plan. "I think we need to go to my father and tell him how we feel."

Jose snorts loudly. "Hah!" he says. "Your father would never agree to you being with me." His gorgeous brow furrows with those dark, winged eyebrows drawn together. Then he raises those eyebrows and excitedly says, "Unless I were to show him I'm just as good as the guy he thinks you're going to marry."

Judith now has hope in her voice as she asks, "How?"

"I could tell my father I'm through with picking apples and then I could enroll in college with you. We could continue going to school and I could get a better job making more money. That's how!"

"That's just what I was hoping you'd say, Jose. Now my father can't have a leg to stand on if he tries to criticize you. Oh, you've made me so happy!"

Jose again draws her close and places his chin atop her head, staring off into the beauty that surrounds them on this crisp autumn day. Quietly, he says, "I do love you Judith, and it will all work out. I know it."

Leaning her head back and looking up at him, Judith looks deep into his eyes, seeing his love for her reflected there. She nods her head, leans in for a soft kiss, and then says, "Come on. Let's go find my father. He should be having lunch now." She giggles. "That's not all he'll be having. He'll probably have a coronary. But we've got a plan, and I think it might just work."

She puts her arms around Jose's waist and they sink to the fragrant blanket of fallen apples under the tree. "But, first . . . ." Judith says. And then there's no more talking.

COCKAMAMIAN COCKROACH

"**G**OOD GRIEF, THAT is one nasty looking bug!" Bitsy exclaims, shuddering delicately.

Bobby says, "Yeah, but I bet he couldn't hurt you if he tried."

"Well, he just better not try!" Bitsy casts a last disgusted look at the cockroach before they continue with their tour of the jungle. They are here on their honeymoon in the depths of Madagascar and seeing things unimaginable to such city-bred neophytes.

Lying in their sleeping bags in their tent pitched under a canopy of trees deep into the jungle, they talk about how vicious the cockroach sounded when he hissed. Soon asleep, Bitsy begins to dream about a huge, preying cockroach that is terrorizing a small city. She feels something crawl across one of her exposed legs. Thinking she is still deep in her dream, she ignores it. But when it begins crawling across her other leg, she knows this is not a dream. "Bobby!" she shrieks. "Something's in my sleeping bag!"

She instinctively reaches down and slaps her leg where the crawling sensation is. "Quick, get a light," she yells.

She brings her hand up to her face in the wan light the lantern provides and sees the goop dripping between her fingers. "Yecchhh!" she cries out loudly. This is followed by gagging noises as her dinner, hot dogs cooked over the open fire, climbs back into her throat.

"Can I help?" Bobby asks. Mirth and disgust alternately play on his face.

"Damn straight!" she gasps. "Get this bag off me so I can see what's under there."

Bobby pulls it away from her. They both look at her naked thigh and gag. Lying there, smashed flat with its yellow, gooey insides spread across it, is the biggest cockroach either has ever seen. It's at least an inch longer than the big male they had seen that afternoon.

Before they can even get a tissue to wipe it up, another cockroach crawls from beneath the discarded sleeping bag and runs quickly up Bobby's stomach. Bobby slams his hand against the offending bug and flattens it completely. When he takes his hand away they see that even its head is crushed and is leaking greenish-yellow goop.

His eyes wild, Bobby spots a towel used for his bath that evening and wipes it first across Bitsy's thigh and then his stomach. He turns it over and there lie the remains of the two cockroaches.

His eyes change to a gleam as a thought takes shape in his head. "I know what let's do," he says, a smile starting on his lips.

Her face still screwed up in distaste, Bitsy asks, "What?"

"Let's smuggle the disgusting things back. We can show them off and then eat them, that's what!"

"Eat them?" Bitsy echoed. "Are you crazy?" Turning her head to the side, she adds, "I think I'm going to be sick."

"No, listen," Bobby says, really getting into his plan, "this could be great fun. Sort of like that guy on TV who eats all that yucky crap. Let's do it!"

Reluctantly, Bitsy agrees, thinking she might rethink her future plans with Bobby.

With the cockroaches stowed with a small chunk of dry ice inside a tampon tube inside her makeup kit, Bitsy breezes through airport security. Once home, they invite two couples, good friends, for dinner. All are eager to taste this new culinary treat that Bobby has dubbed Madagascar Cockamamie.

Bobby and Bitsy had set about concocting a dish around the two cockroaches, their spilled insides still appearing as oozy fresh as the moment they had been slapped out of them. "Well, there's a dish called Bahamian Conch and another called Panamanian Black Snapper – why don't we call this one Cockamamian Cockroach? Everybody will just think it's a bunch of cockamamie, anyway."

Bitsy agreed, thinking that was a super name for the dish. She is finally really getting into the game.

Preparing the dish, she layers some potatoes in the bottom of a baking dish, pours in a can of diced tomatoes, adds some sliced onions and green pepper, and shakes salt and pepper over it all. She places the two cockroaches in the middle and spoons the juice over them. "I think 375 for 45 minutes ought to do it," she says.

The guests arrive right on time, each hungry for a delicious new evening meal. Bobby directs everyone to sit at the dining table. Smiling sweetly, Bitsy places the hot dish in the center of the table while Bobby opens a bottle of Chardonnay.

Sandra dips in a spoon, then gasps and asks, "Is that what I think it is, Bitsy?"

"Yep," Bitsy replies, a huge grin spreading across her face.

They all peer at the dish. "Well, hell, I ain't gonna eat no roach," Bud roars.

"Yes, we all are," Bobby says seriously. "It's delicious. Bitsy and I ate it almost every day while we were in Madagascar."

"That's right! So we brought some home to prepare for you guys," Bitsy agrees. "It tastes exotic. You'll love it. Green pepper and onion! Just try it and you'll see. In fact Bobby will try our version of the dish first." She nods at Bobby.

Bobby ladles a bit onto his plate, being sure to take a piece of one roach's hindquarters. Grinning, he puts the bite of roach into his mouth. He immediately shudders, his whole body in spasms. Then his mouth opens and the bite of Cockamamian Cockroach spews forth across the table.

George jumps up, his chair skidding backward. He claws at his face, he gags, and quickly loses his lunch before sitting down with a thump.

Gloria screams. "One's moving; I can see it! Oh God, it smells rotten," she says, just before turning to the side and throwing up in Bitsy's plate.

Sandra and Bud jump up and run for the kitchen sink, holding their hands over their mouths. Sandra doesn't make it. Thankfully, Bud does.

Bitsy stands with hands on hips and surveys the chaotic scene around her. "Don't be such wussies," she says as she frowns at Bobby.

She calmly inserts a fork into one of the roaches and lifts it to her mouth. She chews. She reaches with her fork for a bite of tomato and potato, and into her mouth these go to join the roach. She chews again. She will be damned before she gets sick in front of all these people they have decided to play a joke on. Bobby is such a wimp!

"All it needed was the vegetables to go with it. It tastes divine. Mmmmm-Mmmmm!"

EITHER THE FIGS GO OR I DO

I GREW UP on a farm with fig trees. I know what a fig tree does. It's once again fig season and I'm excited! For the last three years, since we moved on to this property, our lone fig tree hasn't seemed to know what it is supposed to do when fig season occurs or even what fig season is all about. It's a lovely tree, and we had high hopes for it to bear fruit. In the spring it always thrust out buds that soon unfurled into large, lush leaves. The kind of leaves Adam could have worn comfortably as he left the Garden of Eden. Fig leaves are big enough to cover a lot of things.

With the advent of spring this year, our seemingly slumbering tree awakes. It puts on its usual full cloak of vibrant green leaves and seems to grow to three times its size as they cover its bare limbs. Soon little nubs poke forth all over the tree, including its lower limbs that all but brush the ground. Not long after the nubs appear, little green balls burst out. These grow at an alarming rate for a couple of weeks.

We wait for the busy little gray squirrels to render the tree figless, as they had joyfully and fearlessly done every year (not hungrily, for we fed the little scavengers every day) to our two peach trees whose branches hung low, barely able to hold up the weight of so much fruit. This year one last solitary peach hung from the very end of the tallest and thinnest of branches. It drove the squirrels nuts! They couldn't reach it. No matter how they contemplated and cogitated, it eluded them. As one after the other of the squirrels met his match, we thought we might salvage just *one* peach from this year's crop. A squirrel would cautiously tread the limb, thinking dinner was at hand. Then the branch would bend under the weight and the squirrel would either fall off or have to rapidly backtrack to prevent doing so. I think the squirrels finally worried the little peach until it just gave up the ghost and fell off. It's possible that one enterprising squirrel may have figured out a way to snag it, but I like to think not.

Our fig tree isn't a complete dummy; it did manage to put out a couple of figs each year. Whether it was the squirrels, the birds, disease, or simply gravity, none of the figs matured. Whoa! Not so this year! I can't believe one fig tree, let alone one who wasn't entirely sure it *was* a fig tree, could possibly have so much fruit. Its branches that almost brushed the ground do so now, liberally dripping figs. Every branch is loaded and sagging with the tiny-seeded fruit.

Every day I go out armed with a large wicker basket. I set the basket on the ground and start picking large, ripe, brown figs which are ready to burst and share their velvety goodness. These go into the basket. But wait! There's more way up high. So I get a hook set on a long pole and attack again, and this time I am able to pull down the branches low enough so that by standing on tip-toe and reaching way up high, I can snare those succulent teasers. Into the basket they go. More follow. Soon I have a basketful. Now what am I going to do with all these figs? Back home when I was growing up, Mama made delicious fig preserves, which we then ate on toast every morning of our lives. But, what should *I* do?

Let's see, I have given them away to neighbors, friends, and relatives, made many, many batches of fig preserves, and gave those away also. I've used them in green salads, made several versions of fresh fig cake, and eaten them straight from the tree while they were still warm and fragrant. These last were the ones so ripe that they had split open, showing their tender fuchsia insides. Unfortunately, my neighbors, friends, and relatives all appear to be on vacation when I approach their homes with fig basket in hand. Funny – they never tell me they plan to be away.

The tree shows no signs of abating. More little fig babies appear as I pick the ripe ones. I head out today for my usual foray into the green depths with basket handle over my arm. I optimistically state that I don't think there'll be so many today since I picked so many yesterday. I return with my basket brimming. My husband takes one look and says, "Diana, either the figs go, or I do!"

I decide I've made my last fresh fig cake of the year. I suppose I've had my husband far too long to even consider life with figs in it, but not him. Besides, who would fertilize and water my prize fig tree?

MULHOLLAND MAYHEM

I N QUICK SUCCESSION, three shots echoed through the ravine. Bang, bang, bang. The sound resonated far into the tall hills surrounding the dry gulch. Bob and Betty abruptly stopped, heads up, listening, their hiking trip temporarily forgotten. "Hey, did you hear that?" Bob asked.

"That sounded like gunshots. I wonder who's shooting out here?" Concern was etched on her face.

"The question is: what are they shooting? There are no wild animals left."

They were exploring along Mulholland Drive, the winding road that leads from the Pacific Ocean right into the heart of Los Angeles, and had been enjoying this spring outing in the sun. Now, gunshots!

"You know, it could be possible that they're filming a movie," Bob continued.

"That's true, but I don't see any kind of activity or hear any other sounds, like the camera guys, lighting trucks, and stuff like that." Betty said.

"It sounded like the shots came from that direction," Bob said, pointing. "Want to check it out?"

"I don't know, Bob. I'm not sure we should get involved. If it is something bad, I mean."

"We won't know that until we've investigated, will we? Let's go see what we can find. Maybe it'll be nothing. But then, someone may need our help."

"Okay, we'll at least see if we can find where the shots came from."

"We better go this way," Bob said, ducking under the tall, thick brush of mesquite plants. They trekked over small hills and thrashed their way through springtime's profusion of shoots and blooms.

"Better watch out for snakes," Bob warned. "I just read in the Los Angeles Times that rattlesnake season just started."

"Do they normally live around here?"

"They're all over this area. I wish I'd thought about that before I suggested we take this hike."

"Yeah, and we'd have come prepared with a gun," Betty mused. "I can shoot a gun. Did I ever tell you that?"

"Hey, maybe that's it!" Bob responded. "Maybe that's what the gunshots were all about!"

"About me shooting a gun? What are you talking about?"

"No, Silly. I'm talking about the rattlesnakes. Maybe somebody was shooting at a rattlesnake!"

"Well, if it had been me, I would've hit it," Betty asserted,

They crested a hill and looked down into the ravine and saw a body lying on its back behind a large Eucalyptus tree.

"Quick, Betty! Help me," Bob yelled back over his shoulder as he raced down the hill. Betty scrambled along behind Bob and soon they leaned over a middle-aged man whose face was quite red and badly swollen, and who was gasping for breath. A logo on his shirt read "Los Angeles County Parks Department".

"Sir? Sir?" Bob said as he shook the man's shoulder. "Can you tell us what happened?"

"Snakebit," the man gasped. "Over there . . . behind you."

"It *is* a snake! And it sure looks like he's dead!" Betty tugged her cell phone from the pocket of her shorts and punched in 911.

"Where'd he get you?"

"Neck. Tripped, fell down."

"You'll be okay, Sir. The ambulance is coming."

"Thanks," the man said, and gave a tiny squeeze to Bob's hand.

Betty said, "Mister, you must be a dead-eye shot! We heard three shots and this snake is blown into three different pieces. Good job!"

She added under her breath, "I couldn't have done better myself!"

AH, ENGLAND!

M Y DAUGHTER, ELIZABETH, had just graduated from college. I was such a proud mother and I wanted to do something special for her huge achievement. She had done these last two years on her own, without monetary assistance from her family, and I felt she deserved something big! Remembering her interest in Britain when I went there years ago, I thought the perfect thing to do would be to treat her to a trip to the UK with me. She was exceedingly excited at the prospect, so I began to make plans. I bought an English Bed and Breakfast book and a touring guide and perused them cover-to-cover, planning our entire trip and where we would stay. Then I began the round of international phone calls to check for availability and to make reservations.

Elizabeth flew from Wisconsin to Washington, DC and we flew out together that evening on our over-night flight to Heathrow Airport in London. We both tried to sleep, each stretching out on three seats in the under-booked plane. Darn those arm rests that don't fold completely back! They dug into my back, my side, anything that touched them. Elizabeth, who could sleep through any natural act of God-earthquakes, hurricanes, tornadoes, you-name-it-had a good deal more success than I.

Aaaahhh, London! So much to see and do. I retraced many of my previous steps, this time with Elizabeth. We left our luggage in the "left luggage" room at the airport and took the tube in to the city. Spending the day visiting all the typical sights was great fun, but we comprised a tornado of activity, and to say it was a tad bit tiring was like saying the Thames River was a tad bit wet. I was too excited, being in one of my favorite places on earth, to be entirely exhausted, yet my sleepy-head Elizabeth fell asleep riding atop one of the red double-decker buses on our way to the Tower. Long lines and too many people put the nix on getting in to see the Crown Jewels, but she was impressed with the tower and the stories of imprisonment. Afterward, we walked for miles throughout the heart of the city, ogling everything, including Harrods' department store, Trafalgar Square, and Piccadilly Circus, and thoroughly enjoying our day in London. We had lunch in the St. Martin In the Field church basement. It is now far from any field, but continues its custom of preparing lunches. We had the wonderfully delicious cooked vanilla custard over a marvelous bread pudding.

We returned to Heathrow by the tube, retrieved our left luggage and picked up our rental car. Smiling engagingly and talking earnestly, the salesman was able to make us see the error of our ways in reserving the least expensive car and we walked out, contract in hand, to a larger, more comfortable, and more stylish vehicle. Elizabeth insisted her reflexes were better than mine, and since she'd had more sleep, (falling asleep on the double-decker was a good thing, she said) her brain wasn't as fogged, so she won the opportunity to be the first to drive on the wrong side of the road in the wrong side of the car. Within a few blocks of the rental car lot, she was driving like a native. After spending the night in our first B&B outside of London, and taking the wheel myself the next day, I found it was a piece of cake and was soon driving a zillion miles an hour like the other fools. Why? Because we *could!* The speed limits on their big highways aren't set at seventy, like ours. So, I floored it and took off for Stonehenge, admiring the scenery with every mile. Once there, Elizabeth walked all around the site, head thrown back, staring at each of the huge stones, but I chose not to, viewing it from outside the fence, since I had picked up a good case of blisters walking all around London the day before. Awesome to behold! Stonehenge, not the blisters, though some of them were rather sizable.

Who built something of this magnitude? It's still the unanswered question.

Winchester Cathedral proved to be a wonder. Seeing the entombments in the floor or wall of Jane Austen and other notables was amazing. Elizabeth had not seen this particular way of burial before touring Westminster Abby and it was still taking some getting used to. We had trouble finding the cathedral, though we could see it above the trees when exiting the car park and we stood on the sidewalk looking at a map and trying to figure out which road, for Pete's sake, that we would take to get to it. A man happened by and asked if he could help. At Elizabeth's explanation of what we were trying to do, he plucked the map from her hand, said, "Bloody hell!" and folded it up and gave it back to her. Most assuredly he was thinking more idiotic tourists, but he said, "Go down to the monument at the end of the way and turn left. You can't miss the bloody thing!" We did, and there it was!

We passed some of the most gorgeous scenery imaginable as we headed out to the very tip of England at Land's End. The lush green fields with their stone surrounds were captivating. We stopped and had our first English Tea of scones and strawberry jam with their famous Devon clotted cream at a little roadside tavern in Devon. Elizabeth was hooked, and after that we looked for places in the afternoons where we could stop and have a spot of tea.

On through Cornwall we drove, where we saw enormous blue hydrangeas the size of VW vans, and we finally pulled into our ancient B&B, set right on the water of the Atlantic on the *other* side with which we were familiar.

I had to put my feet in that fishy smelling water, of course, walking into the waves in my sandals. Within seconds of getting out of the water, they smelled so bad until we relegated them to the boot and put our luggage on the back seat. When we next opened the boot, thinking they would have dried out and the odor would've gone away, we were sadly mistaken; the smell just about knocked us over. The odor of dead fish pales in comparison. Slamming the boot shut and about to retch, we looked for a refuse bin and eventually found one alongside the road, in which we gratefully dumped the sandals.

Driving through the Cotswolds, we spied a farm down a hillside in an idyllic setting. I slammed on the brakes and Elizabeth hopped out and navigated precariously down the hillside to get closer so she could take a picture of it. Later, after a gigantic, and absolutely delicious, dinner of fish and chips purchased at the nearby pub, we stayed that night in a lovely little B&B in Stratford on Avon, with flowered wallpaper that matched the bedspreads. We met two girls, American college students backpacking around England, at breakfast the next morning, which brought a brief wave of nostalgic longing for home. It was a full English breakfast, mind you. Fried eggs, their version of bacon (ham to us), mushrooms (either fresh or canned), tomato (either freshly broiled, or straight from the can) and toast. Lots of jams and jellies and a variety of cereals always accompanied this.

On our tour that day, Elizabeth was as mightily impressed with Anne Hathaway's house as was I the first time I saw it. Imagine the young William Shakespeare courting her there on the same bench on which we sat! The Cotswolds were full of thatched-roof cottages, but that house was one of the finer examples.

After driving north into Scotland we spent a night at an inn that William Wordsworth's family had once owned. We climbed the creaky stairs to our room, and stared with wonder at the sheep grazing in the field just below our open window. This night came with its own special effects as we were blasted with an emergency-indicating horn and found ourselves out in the courtyard with the other puzzled guests, not once, but twice. It turned out to be a malfunctioning alarm system. Whew! We truly lucked out on that one! No way could we have navigated the rickity warren of halls and stairs had there been a real fire.

Elizabeth and I took more time at the Old Castle in Edinburgh than I had done before, so we saw lots more of the impressive heap. We looked out over the Firth of Forth, as the body of water below was called, from our spot atop the high wall. We both could claim to having driven on at least a part of the Royal Mile, since I drove *in* to the town and found a carpark, and she drove *out* on our way back to England.

That night was spent in a B&B run by the friendliest folk we had ever met. Alas, Elizabeth's stomach had rebelled from eating "The Full English Breakfast" every morning, so she requested only muffins and cereal. The one morning we had blood sausage and kippers added to our by now standard full English breakfast, she almost lost it. Literally. She turned green and gagged. I, being me, Miss Try Anything Once, tried each. I had to admit the blood sausage was exceptionally foul. The kippers weren't anything to write home about, either.

When we left, with hugs all around from our hosts, we took a quick trip out to look at Hadrian's Wall in the pouring rain, which was, astoundingly, the only bad weather we encountered on the trip. Yes, it was there, at least the remnants of it, this wall separating the barbarian heathens of the north, in Scotland, from the more refined and cultured people of England.

Returning to the London area we went through Lincoln. Right across the street from the huge cathedral we had tea with all the accompaniments in the cellar of what once was a dungeon in the 1200s. We stopped off at Oxford and, naughtily and with great stealth, opened one of the huge gates to King's College and peeked around. Then next, on an impulse, we drove to Princess Diana's home, thinking we would just take a look at where the privileged people lived and where she had grown up and where she was now buried. Unbeknownst to us, the house was open for the first time since her death for tours. We stood outside the gates and watched the people who had tickets go in to tour the house. We were content to watch from behind the wall surrounding the property and take pictures of each other with the grand house in the background. When leaving, we drove down the lane past the very gate that the funeral procession bringing Diana's body home had ended and where massive banks of flowers had been placed. Elizabeth and I had, along with most of the world, watched the procession as we sat transfixed in front of our TV's.

Our last night in England was spent in another very accommodating B&B in the shadow of the huge, looming Windsor Castle some miles from London. I was thrilled to find Queen Elizabeth's standard was not flying atop the castle, which meant she was not in residence there and we could tour it. Wow! Tour it we did, shoulder to shoulder with all the other tourists. It was quite an experience to shuffle along, turning my head from side to side in awe and admiration, but hardly being able to breathe in the unseasonable heat and what seemed to be half the population of Europe walking along beside me. Elizabeth and I agreed we were both glad we had done it, having never seen any residence so richly appointed, or as large! Queen Elizabeth had been in residence at Buckingham Palace when we saw it from outside the fence the day we'd spent in London, and we surely were glad she'd decided to stay there.

"Mom," Elizabeth said, grinning impishly at me, "this is the most magnificent country in the world! I'm so pleased you thought to give me this as a graduation gift. Thank you, thank you, thank you!"

"You're most welcome. It was definitely my pleasure. I love England, too!"

She covered with the light coverlet on her bed and was soon asleep. I began my preparations for bed in my twin across the room. Suddenly she sat straight up in bed and said, "Except for home! There's no place as great as home!" She paused. "But England is a close second."

I looked around at the pink and white bedroom of our B&B. I knew this last night spent in splendid comfort, after such an amazingly hot, tiring day, would prove to be a grand end to this trip to England. It would not be my last. Ah, England! She beckons seductively and we, her bewitched, return again and again. It was a perfect end to a perfect trip. But, Elizabeth is right, I thought. Home, with all that it entails, is where she truly belongs.

A corner of my heart will remain in England, however. I know this because it is England where my heart takes flight. It is England where the instant I leave London and head for the countryside, I feel like I've come home. It is England in which I experience an aura enveloping me that says "You not only have been here before but you've *lived* here before. Many years ago and in another life."

I think that perhaps I was once a milkmaid on one of the lush farms in the rolling hills of Dover. For it is here that my heart has a special affinity for the surroundings. Its green fields surrounded by stone walls speak to my heart. And it says, "Yes," in return.

STOP OR I'LL SHOOT

"**S**TOP OR I'LL shoot!" Liza over-emotes.

"Cut," Todd, the director yells. "Cut, cut, cut!"

Todd strides across the lot at Tantamount Studios, shoving aside a camera-man here and a key-grip there. His destination is all too obvious as his gaze fixes firmly on the lovely Liza's now fear-filled face.

"What did I tell you about that crap, Liza? Do I have to get someone to replace you in this role?" he demands, red-faced with anger.

"Uhhh . . . ."

"Damn right," he continues, giving his young ingénue star no chance to complete her sentence. Good thing, because she has no idea what to say.

"I told you to act natural, to act like a real pro, not to act like Joan Crawford or any of those old Hollywood stars. You need to act like *today*, talk like *today*, sound like *today*, not like you're overdoing it. Which you are!" He stalks off, then whirls and adds, "Let's try it again. For the umpteenth time. This time you better nail it!"

In a most foul mood, he takes his high director's chair seat. "From the top," he says to the camera-man. "You too, Liza."

Liza takes a deep breath, tries her zoning-out method to clear her head, opens her eyes again and says earnestly to Todd, "I'm ready. I think I've got it this time."

The scene opens with the ubiquitous intruder climbing through Liza's (now Norah's) open bedroom window. Its opening has only a tiny slit at the bottom, but it's obviously enough for the assumed burglar/rapist/up-to-no-gooder as he wedges his fingers under the window and lifts it up and open from his handy perch on the fire escape outside the window.

Norah is standing in the adjoining room, her small living room/dining room combination, setting the table for two, when she hears the slight but distinct noise from the window being slid up. Quickly, her brow a study in concentration, she whips across the small space to the computer desk. She first picks up a letter opener and assesses it. Her lovely mouth pouts and she whispers, "No good."

Todd can see her acting as if she is desperately thinking of what she can possibly use against the intruder, her face lined in terror, her eyes glistening with tears.

"Cut," Todd shouts. "Your body language and range of emotion is good here. That's much better than before, Liza. Now, I want you to show that you are really thinking about what you're about to do, and you're agonizing over it. After all, you are about to shoot someone."

"Okay, Todd," Liza replies, secretly pissed at him for interrupting what she thinks is a great job, and now its continuity is ruined.

"From the cut to Liza at the table," Todd directs to James, the very tired camera-man, who's been at this for over eight hours now. He thinks Liza is doing just fine. He is so ready to call it a day and go get cleaned up so he can meet his date at their favorite bar.

"Right," he says, dutifully aiming the camera at Liza, who is again standing at the dining room table, plate in hand, ready to set the table.

"Annnnd action!" Todd yells.

Norah places the plate just so on the table. She looks at it and decides it is fine, lips upturned in a half-smile. She nods slightly and turns to the small sideboard where more plates, silverware, and stemmed glasses sit. She hears the sound of the window opening, shock and disbelief registering on her face, and then quickly she crosses to the computer desk. No, the letter opener won't do. Tears form in her eyes. What to do now? Her face is a mask of terror and, along with her hesitation, portrays indecision.

"I can't do it," she says in a barely audible whisper, breathing out the words on a sigh of despair. "I hate guns!" she says a little more strongly. However, she hesitantly slides open the bottom right drawer of the desk. The camera pans to its depths. There lies a hand gun atop the papers in the drawer. Pan back to Norah's face, which now struggles deeply with indecision. She picks up the gun, her delicate features drawn into a knot in the middle of her face, as she wrestles with her moral dilemma.

From the director's chair, Todd mutters to himself, "Okay, okay, just go with it Liza." This is much better, he thinks.

Suddenly, Norah sprints into her bedroom. She squeezes her eyes shut at the last instant as she swings around the door, gun pointed straight in front of her, held with both hands. Adrenalin pumping she shouts, "Stop, or I'll shoot, you asshole!"

Todd almost fell off his chair. "Keep rolling," he hissed to James the camera-man. This is certainly "today" at its best, he thought.

Curt, the actor playing the role of Jake, Norah's boyfriend, freezes in mid-stride. He is between the window and the bedroom door, so is standing about five feet from Norah. He stops with a jerk, flings his hands into the air, and exclaims, "Don't shoot, Norah. Dammit, it's me, Jake."

"Ja-a-ke?" Norah stutters out, her face now radiating disbelief, her voice weak and surprised.

Good job, thinks Todd.

"Well, damn it, it is your birthday and I wanted to surprise you!" His voice is shaky, his face a landscape of surprise as he stares at the gun pointing at him.

Todd is thrilled as he watches a look of relief replace the fear and surprise on Liza's face, reacting to this surprising, scary intrusion by someone she knows and loves. Just like he told her to do.

Todd watches anger spreads across Norah's face, the relief melting beneath it. Her eyes blaze, her face flushes, and she darts to Jake, draws her hand back and slaps his left cheek with great force.

"You damn well did!" she shrieks as the blow lands. "What the crap were you thinking, you idiot? I could have shot you! Why couldn't you come through the front door instead of trying to sneak in the window?"

Reeling from the slap, Jake staggers slightly. His reaction is real, not just scripted, so all the more believable. Recoiling from the slap, Jake puts his hand up to his face and gently touches his cheek.

His voice deadly, Jake says, "It's a damn good thing you didn't shoot me. I had no idea you had a gun – you, of all people, with your holier than thou attitude against people who own guns. Where in hell did you get a gun?" His face is screwed up in distaste.

"Hey, don't turn it back on me." Disgust is written on her features as she hurls this dictate back at him. "You're the one who scared hell out of me first. So, the gun scared you a little bit, so what? You intruded into my home. I could have shot you and you could be dead right now."

Todd can hardly contain himself; he is so pleased with the turn this has taken. Sure, they were following the dialogue, but Liza's delivery and actions were so much better than they'd ever been before. Whoa, wait a minute! He saw realization spread across Norah's face. It looked as if she had an idea. This was not in the script. What was she doing?

Norah says to Jake, "In fact, I could kill you right now and no one would know it wasn't an accident."

Jake realizes Norah is adlibbing and decides to play along. A quick glance at Todd shows him to be leaning forward in his seat, intrigued.

"Yeah?" he questions.

Todd signaled for James to keep shooting film. A circular roll of his fingers near his ear indicates "keep going."

Sighing, James does.

"In fact, I might just do that," Norah says, her eyes narrowed and her lips tight. "It'd serve you right for running around on me with that piece of trash Kelly."

"What, uh, what do you mean?" Jake lets fear and innocence wage war all over his face and body. His eyes look down, his shoulders slump. "I haven't done anything to Kelly. Hell, I don't even know Kelly." He extends a hand toward Norah and pleads, "Baby, you know I wouldn't run around on you. I love you."

Anger and determination turn Norah's face into flint. "Bullshit," she so unladylike says. "You don't love me and I don't love you." In a nano-second, she raises the gun from where it had been pointing to the floor until it now points straight at Jake's chest. Her face radiates cool calm, but her eyes flash anger.

"Goodbye, Jake," she says lightly, and lifts her head, strongly and proudly. She stares into his terror-filled eyes for a brief moment. The camera-man pans away from her face to her finger tightening on the trigger. As Norah's finger pulls the trigger, he pans back to Jake's face, wide with surprise and hurt. He crumples to the floor, hand pressed against his chest.

She brings the gun up before her eyes,and with her lips now spread in a delighted smile, Norah says, "Who says I don't like guns? Why, they're life-savers. At least for me."

Liza turns to Todd and gives him an impish "I'm sorry I got so carried away" grin while shrugging her shoulders endearingly.

Todd is now half in love with his leading lady. Who knew she could improvise like that? Of course it would mean shooting the correct scene yet again, but Liza had proved she had some real talent. Talent that he had been unsure he would ever discover in her. Whew! He is not going to have to recast her role after all!

"Okay, Liza," he says. "That was quite a show. Good job, however." To Curt he said, "That was brilliant to play along with her. I hope that's the last time she will feel the need to do that. I think that now she will be able to portray her role just fine."

Liza blushes daintily, almost deliriously happy that her brainstorm had not back-fired.

Todd looks around the assorted crew and says, "That's a wrap for today. Come back at six o'clock in the morning ready to work!"

James finishes buttoning up his camera and turns to Liza. "Ready to go, Hon? Let's go have a beer. We might still have time for that date later. But, no guns, okay?"

LEFT OR RIGHT

GURGLE, GUR-GLE, GURRR-GGGLLLE. The sound came from beneath her. Frightened by the mysterious sound, Jillian jumped straight up from her seat.

Just minutes earlier, Jillian lay sound asleep in her bed, snuggled deep beneath the soft sheets and warm duvet. She was deep into a dream about the dinner party she was planning for the coming weekend. Several prominent people from the country club would be attending. It was to be her first effort in immersing herself into the close-knit group who lived in her heavily wooded lake community. She was very apprehensive about making the cut. She was becoming agitated in the dream as she saw her table settings slide off onto the floor and the sink in the kitchen that was filled with dirty pots and pans over flow. She watched in dismay as the water ran across the tile floor of the kitchen and out into the hall. It began to wet the hall carpet, inching to the front door just as the doorbell rang announcing the first guests. She was thankful when a full bladder and the need for relief woke her.

With her cozy, long flannel nightgown trailing on the plush carpet of her newly finished bedroom and bath, Jillian, yawning, made her way to the bathroom. She sat down on the toilet and quickly relieved the pressing need that had awakened her. She was preparing to rise when she heard the first of the gurgles. That's the only way she could think to describe the noise. She shot up from the toilet seat and listened in horror as the terrible sound continued.

Looking down into the toilet bowl she could see, by the faint light afforded by the slitted-open vertical blinds that covered the bathroom's large windows, that the bowl's water was roiling. She took an involuntary step backward, which proved to be a wise move, just as an object of dubious make erupted from the depths of the toilet, slinging droplets of dirty water all about.

The object, the critter, the creature from the depths, whatever it was, literally flew to the window, drawn by its dawning light, and perhaps the hope of freedom, and began to bat itself against the blinds in a frantic, but futile, effort to escape. Jillian, now immensely frightened, still had the presence of mind to retreat to her bedroom and to jump on to her bed. She sought what safety it afforded by being raised off the floor. The floor that she had a dreadful feeling the creature would soon find.

The animal, for Jillian had now determined that it had to be some kind of animal, streaked down the hall and past her bed where she huddled against the headboard with the duvet clutched in her hands like a frail shield. She glimpsed the critter as it passed her and she saw that it was thin of body with a long tail and its hair was wet with strings matted and strands standing out all around its body. As this registered in her terrified brain, the animal began to fling itself against the vertical blinds that faced the lake and where the light coming in was marginally brighter.

After about a minute, it dropped to the floor and raced about under the windows and past the door that opened to the large wooden deck.

SHE IS WOMAN - COURAGEOUS, COMPELLING, AND CAPTIVATING - (AND SOMETIMES OUTRAGEOUS!)

| 115

Jillian's frozen brain had a moment of clarity when she realized that if she forced herself to leave the safety of her bed and try to cross behind the animal, she could likely open the door to the deck and the animal might be able to escape her bedroom. This she fervently hoped as she leapt from her bed, and with feet hardly touching the floor, she safely reached the door and gave it a hard yank, sending it crashing back against the wall of windows.

The animal, spooked, jumped high into the air, bashing against the blinds again before it realized the door was open wide and might be an avenue of escape. Once its decision was made to make a run for it, run it did! Straight out the door it raced and fetched up against the hot tub. Regaining its balance, it skittered down the steps to the deck below, stood there a moment while vigorously shaking its body to rid itself of the wetness, and who knows what else, and then scampered across the deck. Jillian's last sure glimpse of the creature was its bedraggled tail disappearing up the trunk and into the leafy greenness of the old live oak tree whose broad limbs shaded the hot tub deck. She wasn't sure, but she thought she could see his sharp little eyes staring at her from the safety of one of the larger limbs.

"What was that?" she wondered aloud. She went back inside and surveyed the chaos. Heaving a great sigh, she got busy doing damage control before the dirty toilet water stained irrevocably her new carpets.

The weekend came, and with it came her dinner party. Guests began arriving and were directed to her bedroom to place coats and wraps on her bed. The freshly cleaned carpets showed no signs of the critter and the ensuing chaos it had wreaked on the new home of which she was so proud. Originally intending to never tell of the occurrence, Jillian found she simply had to know what the creature was and how it got into the depths of her toilet. She decided to tell her story to her guests and see if anyone had any idea to contribute about its identity.

Each guest had filled his bowl with the sumptuous New Orleans gumbo and rice and each had added a spoonful of the file` gumbo to the top. All were taking their seats either at the beautifully appointed dining room table or at the card tables, now unrecognizable as such with their autumn decorations. Soon the meal was underway with Jillian passing baskets filled with slabs of japalena, cheddar, and corn-kernel cornbread. All were exclaiming how delicious the food was and how Jillian was certainly a most welcome asset to the neighborhood. Jillian kept the fine white wine flowing and the conversation became mellower as one and all relaxed with appetites sated and feeling quite comfortable with Jillian and her lovely home.

After Bananas Foster for dessert with a delightful light German dessert wine and a choice of New Orleans Chicory or Ghiradelli chocolate-flavored coffee, everyone began to talk companionably about golf at the country club, how their favorite sports teams were faring, and someone brought the conversation around to hunting, another favorite past time of the area.

With hunting the topic, Jillian saw her opportunity to tell her story about the animal in the toilet. She would conveniently exclude the part about the dirty water and the bedroom carpet. She could perhaps find out what it was. A chipmunk? A rat? A weasel? Having been brought up in a grand old house near the French Quarter in New Orleans and protected from the outdoors lest the relentless sunshine mar her porcelain complexion, Jillian knew little of the animal life of the area.

She relayed her story and the great fear she experienced upon witnessing the thing erupt from the toilet and bat itself against the window blinds and finished with a plea, "Please, someone, can you tell me what on Earth the thing could've been?"

At the earnest look of horror and confusion written across that lovely pale face, the men guffawed and the ladies tittered. Jillian was mortified. She had told her story and asked about the animal because she truly didn't know what it was, and she really needed to know. Seeing her blush of embarrassment, one gentleman tried to alleviate her discomfort.

"Oh, it's all right, Jillian. We're just having a bit of fun with you. You see, I think we all know what it is. It has to be a squirrel."

"Yes, of course it is," one of the wives continued. "They are the nosiest little creatures around. They can get into the most trouble you've ever seen. I'm so sorry you thought we were laughing at you, Jillian. That certainly was not our intent."

"Oh, let me tell you about the time a squirrel did . . . ." and "You wouldn't believe what one of the little buggers did to . . . ." and other stories of the like sprang up around the room.

"But – how did he get down in there?" Jillian asked.

Most turned to look at the oldest gentleman in the group, who was the go-to guy for many of the questions regarding animals in the area. He cleared his throat as if to launch into a long dissertation. Jillian was relieved that he quickly and easily got to the point. "On top of your roof you have a pipe that lets out gases from the septic mound that would otherwise come into the house through the toilet. Your Nosy Norman was exploring on the roof and fell into the pipe. Now that pipe has a "Y" fork in it. If he had gone left on the fork he would've gone on into the septic tank and would have smothered and drowned, having no way out. If he chose the right fork he would come up through the plumbing pipes into the toilet. Now, he had to have asked himself, 'Do I go left or do I go right?' Obviously he made the right choice. He went right and so he came up in your toilet, scared half to death and trying desperately to find a way back out to a place with which he was familiar and where he could breathe. That's the story. That solves your mystery. It was just a squirrel."

Quite seriously Jillian said, "Thank you, Mr. Thompson, for explaining it to me. I'll be sure to watch out for squirrels on the roof. Maybe I'll put something up there to dissuade them from nosing about the pipes."

Soon Jillian was laughing along with her guests about more squirrel shenanigans and forgot she had earlier been embarrassed. When the evening was at an end she received a number of invitations to join one or another of her new friends in a round of golf or in a tennis match or to meet for lunch.

Assured that her dinner party had been a success, Jillian climbed into the warm covers of her bed and murmured, "Thank you, my darling little squirrel, skinny and scary though you may be, for being the reason I've made some new friends this evening. Now, let's have no repeats. Stay off my roof, please!"

She was answered by the sound of small feet scampering above her head.

FOR YOU TO FIND OUT

BLONDE HAIR, NEARLY platinum, sits ratted with tendrils tangled atop her almost beautiful face, saved from that distinction by a broad forehead and pointed chin. The small mouth dangles a cigarette, its plumes of smoke breaking from parted lips now curling at the corners. She assesses Joe Cool, peering up at him in the semi-dark from her barstool with appraising blue eyes large with mascaraed lashes.

"Sure, I'll go with you."

He extends a hand sticky with rum and coke and helps her off the barstool while ogling her thin body in the red dress which appears to be applied with magic marker.

"It's this way," he says, tugging her along, parting the reveling press of flesh closing behind them with every struggling step. They burst from the door into frozen air. He checks her.

"What, no coat?" Joe strips his letter sweater from his body, defenseless now in the hard-nipple cold, and he drapes her thin, goose-pimpled arms and swiftly reddening shoulders.

Passing several large square buildings, red bricks shoring up the sides, he turns the car into the fraternity's asphalt parking lot, pitted and potholed like bunkers on a battlefield.

"We're here." Turning, facing her, he finds her lounging against the passenger door, white wisps rising from her nostrils.

"I see." She's smiling slightly, lifting one corner of her mouth. "Let's do it."

They enter to loud clapping, appreciative whistles, catcalls, suggestive comments, vulgar details, much laughter, and all the frat brothers calling out, "Who's first?"

"I am," Joe Cool yells over the clamor. "I found her, I brought her here, she's mine first." Boos ensue. Laughing, Joe takes her elbow as she stands with hands on nearly nonexistent hips, a knowing almost-smirk playing on her lips, and leads her up the gouged and scarred winding staircase to the floor above. They pass several bedrooms with jeans and random sneakers carpeting the floors and an open-doored, cavernous bathroom sprouting wet towels from its walls and floor.

"In here," says Joe, and she is mildly pleased to find a fourposter queen-sized bed arrayed with covers that at first inspection seem clean enough. A wide V from one side of the bed to the door is bulldozed clear. Joe leads her inside and gallantly raises her in muscular young arms, then eagerly drops her onto the bed. Suddenly upon her, he gives her no opportunity to take control of the encounter, as she would prefer.

She whispers to his bent head, "Slow down, Honey." His tongue nuzzles surprisingly large nipples on her small breasts and he shakes his head no.

She promises, "Take your time; it'll be better."

Joe Cool pants, "No, we've got to hurry; they're all waiting their turns."

Lying back upon the pillows, she spreads her legs and opens her arms and he fills hers with his large body. He shudders, finishing too quickly, and it's time for the next one.

As if dying, experiencing an out-of-body existence, she sees herself take in one after another, bruising her breasts, savaging her vagina, while her ardor flags, but she remains compellingly compliant as each one uses her body.

Dropping her at the off-campus bar where he'd found her with a long cigarette glowing and smoky tendrils spiraling skyward from her ruby lips, Joe remembers his searching eyes lighting on her, knowing she is the one. She, possessing a sexy nonchalance, a certain darkness lurking in her eyes, tells him immediately that she is the one to fulfill his fraternity challenge as he, cocky and so sure of himself, tells her what is required of her.

Her assessing expression never wavers as she agrees with his request.

Now, stepping from his car, she says, "So long, sailor." She gives him a saucy salute with hand to forehead, and saunters through the door of the bar, hips swaying, never looking back.

Joe drives off wondering how any woman can do what she did tonight, however, he's jubilant that she did, knowing they'll be the talk of the fraternity house for weeks to come. Sexual arousal assuaged, Joe Cool is thinking of her in a different way: no longer as an exciting, desirable and sexy vixen—even after the incredible sex. He, indeed, feels her to be quite the slut-taking on eleven men in one evening in such a short time. Remembering his one sexual adventure, ineffectually screwing his high school sophomore girlfriend in the cramped backseat of his compact car, he knows it hardly counts in making him a world-class lover. He's been very careful in hiding that small shard of shame, fearing evisceration by his frat brothers. He hears the church's teachings waging war in his head, telling him she's tainted and leaving him hoping his dick doesn't fall off, even though he was wearing a condom. Desire and disdain battling to the finish like gladiators, he eventually settles on thinking she is a strangely beautiful and talented lover of eroticism and exotic sex. With bemusement he recalls her declining the envelope stuffed with twenty dollar bills he offered her when retrieving her after the last man finished.

She said, "I do this because I like it. Don't belittle me by paying me like some common back-alley whore."

The next morning, awakening in her comfortable queen bed in her airy apartment near campus, looking around at the familiar rooms she calls home and admiring the pinks and pale greens, loving the scrupulously clean linens and little-girl decor of her bedroom, Janice gathers from the other pillow her stuffed monkey, holding it to her chest in a tight hug and wincing at the tenderness of her breasts, occasionally happening from out of the blue, and she wonders why.

Arising from the bed, long pink ruffled nightgown trailing behind, she heads for the bathroom, realizing she has that peculiar ache between her legs again, which seems to always come at the same time as the tender breasts. Janice wonders if the two maladies could somehow be tied together, but finds no possible reason at all why they should. Looking in the mirror, and horrified by the way her hair is plastered to her head, she thinks she looks like something out of Star Trek.

Dressing the toothbrush with a large spurt of minty toothpaste, she finds for some reason she has abominably bad morning breath and thinks it must have been something she ate last night. Pausing, considering last night, she realizes it is another of those times when she simply can't remember what she's done. Still wondering what causes these crazy infrequent episodes, she's considering making an appointment with a doctor. But, say what, she asks herself.

Dressed in a modest skirt and blouse with a belt cinched around her boyish waist, she toasts a piece of bread and lathers it with a thin layer of peach preserves. Daintily nibbling it, she heads off to the nearby church preschool for a day of teaching three- and four-year-olds. Janice is preparing for busy, fulfilling work which she loves.

That evening, hugging her small hips and breasts, a dress as black as sin provocatively displays her wares. Red-tipped toes dangling a spiked high-heel sandal, she sips cool white wine from a fine stemmed glass and waits for tonight's fun and games. Seeing the approaching man through lash-lowered eyes, she lifts a corner of her mouth. Smoke escapes and swirls around her lacquered up do. His eyes fasten on hers. They hold gazes, then his drops as he scans her nearly exposed breasts and small figure. Eyes rising up to meet hers again, he dips his head to the side, thinking, "Are you for real?" He smiles expectantly, anticipation written in the lines on his face.

"Well, hello," she says, lips red, wide and welcoming. "I'm Scarlett. Looking for a good time?"

LIKE AN OSTRICH

H E TRULY WAS tall, dark and handsome, standing six feet
two inches, with thick black hair and the darkest brown eyes that burned
into my very soul when he turned them on me. I stood near him, hoping he
would notice me. My heart all but stopped when he did.

It was registration day for our freshman year at college. The odds
were in my favor for attracting some boy's eye, for I was a girl and in the
minority in this mostly male school. I was lucky, and thrilled, that someone
so handsome would choose to make my acquaintance.

He pulled out a chair at my table, straddled it, deftly plucked the pencil
from my hand, and started filling out the reams, it seemed, of pertinent
papers. My laughing protest brought a torrent of questions from him. We
learned each other's names and he immediately invited me to the freshman
mixer to be held the first Friday night of the semester. He said he had to
make hay while the sun shined, claiming a girl right away, for if not, all the
girls would be taken and he'd have to go through life unattached.

"You wouldn't want that to be my fate, would you, Carolyn?" he asked with a sparkle in his eyes and a heart stopping grin.

I quickly stammered some cliché like, "Well, of course not! We'll have to make sure that doesn't happen." I embarrassed myself further by adding, "And I'll be glad to help see that you find a girl."

I'd never met anyone as handsome as he, and certainly not anyone as confident and self-assured. And charming. All around us girls were shooting me dirty looks, their eyes darting from him to me and back to him, each wishing she had captured his attention.

We became a couple immediately and had an exciting love story. Unfortunately, he continued to direct his charm to the girls who still followed his every move, eating him up with their eyes. Soon he was cheating, seeing some girl or another behind my back. I broke up with him, knowing a broken heart now was better than a betrayal later.

Neither of us could forget the other, so fate intervened and we were back together, and this time our reunion culminated in marriage. We graduated together. We both secured good jobs, and within a few years we had the all-American family of Mom and Dad and son and daughter.

But, his good looks and charm, and the reactions they got from almost any female, led him down the primrose path to deceit, adultery, and finally, divorce. My love for him, that had nearly consumed me, died an anguished death on the day he said he wanted a divorce. He would tell me nothing except he needed to be free after being married for most of his life. It was only after our divorce was final that I found he had been having affairs for years with several women, cheating on all of us. I was devastated by his betrayal, but realized I was lucky to be free from such a charlatan.

I learned to not rely on any one, and in doing so, I discovered my own self-worth. I became confident and competent. I also discovered I really liked who I had become. This new me, instead of always taking a back seat to the man who was my husband, put myself first. I felt attractive and empowered and started having an active social life, first with girlfriends, then fix-ups by friends. I was not looking to have a relationship, but one found me.

He was kind, yet strong. Funny, yet compassionate. Sweet, but no pushover. And he loved me! He really, really loved me. For the first time a man put me first. With this good, considerate and loving man, I rediscovered love and what it means to not only give love, as I'd done in the past, but to receive love that is unselfish.

I feel sorry for my ex. He'll go through life continually searching for that elusive love. I've found it. I only wish my blinders had come off earlier. It's a shame I gave so much of my life and myself to him. I was like an ostrich; I had my head in the sand and my butt in the air and never realized what a vulnerable position it could be.

A SISTER'S PRIVILEGE

I LIE AWAKE again. I lie sleepless every night, so this night is no different from all the nights that have passed in the four months since my brother died. Plans juggle for prominence in my mind, one up high, one down low, one on each side in the periphery of my thoughts. They change tactics and flit from one piece of the puzzle to another, lighting on each just long enough to form the rudiments of a plan and then take flight again. I have so much to do and I am so very tired.

My brother was three years older than I and was my closest companion in childhood.

Though we later lived many miles apart, we saw each other as often as we could throughout our young adult years. Sometimes there were years between visits. Most often I saw him at rare family get-togethers. I won't call them reunions; it was more like gatherings in our older sister's home for holidays, especially Thanksgiving. She had assumed the mother roll after our mother died when I was seventeen and was the baby of the family, and he was twenty. But, not once did he forget to call me on my birthday.

In our younger adult years Jack and I had our own separate lives with our own unique set of responsibilities to our spouses, to our children, to our jobs. Once children were out on their own and retirement settled in, there was more time for Jack and me to recapture that closeness we had shared as kids. Our older sister was flirting with old age dementia and, after a last Thanksgiving dinner at her home where we had all travelled large distances to be there and found her to be worried, confused and forgetful, I took on the yearly responsibility of hosting what was now a combined families Thanksgiving meal. For the next several years Jack made the trip to my house for that occasion. Then the breathing problems hit.

It began with shortness of breath. Soon even a walk to the mailbox, located in his rural neighborhood at the end of a fifty yard drive, both tired him and left him winded as if he'd run one of the races he'd competed in while a star athlete in high school. This malady continued for a couple of years, worsening exponentially until an oxygen tank became his constant companion.

Our older sister was hospitalized with kidney problems that resulted in her going on dialysis for several months. Jack and our older brother came together to visit her and stayed in her home while she was in the hospital. It was there that I saw his deterioration and witnessed the oxygen tubes snaking into each nostril. I knew he "had trouble breathing" but nothing drove it home to my unwilling acceptance until I saw it for myself. It was a wakeup call.

A year later, when he was hospitalized with pneumonia, his wife called to tell me it was quite serious. He might not survive. What? That couldn't be. My brain froze at the thought.

I did have presence of mind to break through my fear and book a flight and waste no time in getting to the hospital.

There I found his wife crying and his estranged children from his first marriage awkward and uncomfortable, there only because guilt beat them

SHE IS WOMAN - COURAGEOUS, COMPELLING, AND CAPTIVATING - (AND SOMETIMES OUTRAGEOUS!)

129

into submission and instilled in them the need to see him one more time. I joined this group, and after showing them it was indeed okay to hug and kiss him, I immediately began to question the doctors, the nurses, and the housekeeping staff, anyone whose attention I could gain for even a few minutes about his prognosis. It was hard to accept what I heard in reply.

It was doubtful he would leave the hospital. It was almost certain he would die within a few days. I looked at the tough guy lying in that hospital bed with oxygen up his nose, tubes hanging out of his arms and hands and connected to a variety of bags which hung from poles that surrounded the head of his bed and I said, "You don't know Jack!"

They didn't. Jack was a fighter harking back to the days when he'd meet in our small southern town's Methodist churchyard for an after school fight with whichever bully had picked on someone that day. Heaven help them if it had been me they chose to needle that day! He was my protector and my hero.

Now, in this hospital, he fought for his life. Even after we were told we had better make funeral arrangements and I cornered his wife and daughter and we sat with Jack to talk about it. I so did not want to face the possibility of losing him and having to deal with it. It seemed, however, no one else was going to do it.

Talk about it we did. No candy coating. I flat out asked Jack what he wanted. He agreed upon cremation with a service at the funeral home in their small town. Greatly relieved a decision had been made, and deeply saddened by the nature of it, his daughter and I went to the funeral home and made all the arrangements. We had no idea it would be an additional sixteen months before we would need their services.

Yes, Jack was a fighter. He went home under Hospice care. For several months I encouraged him in our daily phone conversations to do the exercises from his bed that he needed to keep his arms and legs strong. However, he soon could no longer do them; putting the stretchy strap beneath his foot and pushing down while pulling up from either side was too taxing.

He did have one means of escape from his bedroom in the first year of confinement. His daughter found a used scooter made especially for patients' inside and outside use. With help he could straddle the scooter and maneuver from his bed through the living room and out onto the porch where he could sit and smell the fresh wet air after the rain. In the early months he even took the scooter for a spin on the red clay road in front of his home. The scooter was red and I named it Red Riding Hood. He preferred The Red Baron.

My husband and I flew to visit him for three days about the eleven month mark of his surprising survival and stayed at a motel in town so as not to tire him with constant visiting.

He was elated and filled our hours with many, many tales of the past. Jack was a good story teller for he had a sharp memory and his adventures, both at home growing up and as an adult, were fascinating.

An avid reader of all kinds of literature, he went through books like lightning. He watched boxes of VCR tapes and DVD's. He certainly kept his mind strong and healthy. I regularly sent packages of books from the used book store and off the best seller shelves at Barnes and Noble. Our brother did as well.

As the fifteen month survival date approached I made plane reservations for my husband and me to visit again for Jack was definitely declining. Then a medical problem of our own occurred. My husband had emergency quadruple bypass heart surgery. The plane tickets fell right in the middle of his surgery and his subsequent hospitalization for recovery. Jack wouldn't hear of me coming without my husband, saying he was the one who needed me now. He was right, of course.

I changed my non-changeable and nonrefundable flight and paid a sum to do so. Now I was going to see Jack but we'd just have to accept the loss of Frank's ticket since he most assuredly could not fly so soon after surgery

I packed and prepared for my trip the following week. I talked with Jack on Sunday night, January 22, 2012, and said but a few words, mainly that I loved him and was so sorry he was fighting to breathe and that I would call him the next day.

The next morning I was in the midst of a timely conversation about wills with my husband when he answered the phone. My world fell apart then. It was Jack's wife calling to say Jack had just passed away. She said he told her he couldn't breathe and then he went to sleep and did not wake up. I surmise that the lack of oxygen to his brain and organs mercifully caused a coma-like state. I'm thankful that he didn't spend his last moments choking and gasping for breath.

How did this all come about? This fibrosis of the lungs that literally ate up the space so the air sacs couldn't fill? Jack was a Master Plumber by trade and later was a plumbing supervisor and on-the-job instructor. Over the years he pulled away enough asbestos, lead, and other lung debilitating matter from the toilet and shower renovations his company won bids on to compromise his lungs. Once it starts, it is a progressive disease and there is nothing at this time to stop it, or to even to control it for any amount of time.

We did have the cremation and a lovely service led by the Hospice chaplain who had spent many hours in discussion with Jack about God, Christianity, and various religions. He would have approved. His wife kept the beautiful wooden box we had chosen for his ashes and had most of the contents to do with as she wishes. Those weren't all the ashes, however.

I flew out for the service, changing my ticket again, and met my daughter at the airport. She'd flown in from the other side of the continent to give me the support I needed since my husband still couldn't fly. We arranged with the crematory through the funeral home to save a portion of the ashes. I had a beautiful, small, square bronze-colored marble urn for me and a small, round, jade-colored marble urn for our sister. They put some ashes in each and sealed them for us.

Now, to honor Jack's final wishes: He wanted some of his ashes to be interred as his final resting place, and burial place of record, by our father in the cemetery in the small town in which we grew up. Our father died when I was four and Jack was seven. Our mother remarried and upon her death she was buried in a different cemetery in her father's family plot. Jack wanted some of his remains to also be buried by her grave. While the plot beside our father will have the heavy bronze plaque provided by the US Government for veterans, and will illustrate birth and death dates, there will be no plot by our mother. It is to be a simple small hole dug deep with post hole diggers right by the marble-slab-covered grave, and the little urn with the tiny portion of ashes will be buried there. That way he will rest beside both of his beloved parents.

So why have I not been sleeping and why is it pertinent to this story? It's because I am responsible for seeing these last wishes are carried out. My job is to plan and execute every aspect of this last interment since I am the youngest of Jack's three surviving siblings. It's a bonus that I now live only three and a half hours from the two cemeteries that are about thirty minutes apart.

I am continually planning. Every night as I lie awake with thoughts swimming through my head like salmon fighting their upstream battle, I fill in another piece of the puzzle for the big picture. I have planned and written the order for this graveside ceremony. I will act as greeter, will lead the service and will give the eulogy. I was very close to my brother, knew him well, and knew the stories of both past and present that are important to share with mostly those who knew him when he was growing up and will come for the final goodbye to this hometown boy who left this small spot on Earth only to return to lie in its soil. A diamond in the rough Jack certainly was. Under that tough outer facade lay a perfect, sparkling diamond waiting to be unearthed. For those of us who saw it, we were practically blinded by the light. Shine on for us, Jack. Shine on.

I chose the funeral music, wonderful old hymns we sang as children in the Baptist church. Pat Boone's mellow hushed tones on "Whispering Hope" and Elvis Presley's beautiful and haunting "In the Garden" were first choices. It will end with Il Divo's powerful "Amazing Grace," perhaps the best interpretation of this hymn I've ever heard.

I've planned, shopped for, and organized the reception that will follow in the Methodist church's fellowship hall. Will I have three kinds of sandwiches or only one? Will they eat sushi there? Unlikely. Choose something else. Okay, I assume they will eat chicken wings, even if they're not fried. Maybe meatballs. Certainly cakes and cookies. Perhaps a sliced watermelon. Or a fruit bowl instead. A veggie platter should be okay. Got to have sweet iced tea, for sure. My thoughts whirl and choose and discard continually. Finally I arrive, after many nights of lying tense and wakeful, at a menu for the reception. It would have been the appropriate move to have the reception in the Baptist church's hall but it, unfortunately, was unavailable. Jack and I, as children, had attended many funerals in our Baptist church and not a few in the Methodist church, so a reception either place would be a direct connection to our past.

After the second interment, we will return to the first cemetery and the fellowship hall to dismantle and clean up everything. We'll pack it all into the two family cars and return to our homes those three and a half hours away. I expect we will be physically tired and emotionally exhausted. The planning that haunts my nights will be over. I hope to then be able to sleep. It will be finished. But, for tonight, I lie down in my comfortable king size bed with my husband and listen to his gentle snores begin.

"Annie," I say to myself, "just close your eyes and turn your brain off and go to sleep!" I try, but soon I sigh and begin the turmoil in my head that I just can't make go away. Okay, after we set up the chairs graveside, should we . . . or should we . . . or perhaps we should . . . ?

THE PINK LADIES

T HEY ARE THE Pink Ladies. Annette, Gloria, and Jenny. Annette is the ringleader, if it is still in fashion to call someone a ringleader who dreams up fun things to do, like daring escapades, adventurous trips, and imaginative activities.

Annette is a planner. She makes lists. Lots of lists about just about anything she can imagine. And then she does her best to implement them, whatever the fun, or outrageous, or daring, or dangerous activity might be. She enlists her best friends to participate, and since they adore Annette, they willingly go along. Only occasionally do they have reservations or second thoughts before just shrugging their shoulders, closing their eyes, and jumping in. Sometimes literally.

Annette loves all things "Grease." Heavens, no! Not the kitchen or garage kind of grease. The movie kind. After seeing the movie, starring John Travolta and Olivia Newton John, seven times when it first came out in the theatres when she was thirteen, she devoted her life to being a confirmed "Greasehead."

VCR's and Betas were new to the market and Annette's family was the first on their block to buy one. So, with the VCR ensconced by the big color TV that sat prominently in their family room, Annette waited impatiently for Grease to be released to VCR tape. When it finally happened, years and years later, it seemed to Annette, she was in a perpetual state of bliss.

She was free then to watch it as often as she possibly could, sitting on the burnt orange shag carpet that was the height of elegance and desirability of the time, directly in front of the TV – the better to kiss the screen and pretend she was kissing Danny. Of course, she had to bribe her older brother with her allowance and shoo her younger brother from the room with threats of violence in order to have the VCR and TV to herself. And drat! Wouldn't you just know it? Her dad would come home from work wanting to watch the news right in the middle of the school dance scene, or sometimes earlier than that while Danny was singing "Summer Loving" in one place and Sandy was singing it somewhere else. And then there was always her mom wanting her to set the table for dinner or something. Couldn't all these people see that she was serious?

Now she's a forty-seven year old with her own business located in her home and she doesn't have to answer to anyone but herself, so she can watch it as often as she likes. She really doesn't have to watch it, however, because she can visualize every scene in her head, can sing all the songs, and can repeat the entire dialogue, should anyone ask her to. And they have. And she always delivers.

She is aided in this by her solitude. Her three children are grown and gone and she and her husband had an amicable split a couple of years ago. To replace any need for companionship, she relies heavily on the friendship of her two best buddies: Gloria and Jenny. The three spend hours together, which to them often seem all too short. Sometimes they lounge quietly, and soberly, watching a movie from Red Box or Netflix, their favorite genre being the beautifully filmed English romances set in the bucolic English countryside of the 1800's, a la Jane Austen.

Sometimes they don expensive looking evening wear, which they buy from Ross and other discount houses at a fraction of the designer labels' original costs. They rent a limousine and driver for the evening and go to the opera or to a play, usually one that is Broadway bound, so they can claim to have seen it when it was still in its infancy before making it big. The limo's bar is well stocked, of course, and they are usually bombed well before making their majestic exit from the limo in the drive of the theatre.

"Oh, damn! Was that a heel I just broke?" was an all too familiar cry as one or the other stumbled forward with a stiletto heel caught in the hem of her long, elegant, and billowing, gown. Laughing at themselves and ignoring the onlookers, they enter the theater.

They booked cruises twice a year, and had so far visited by cruise excursion most of the places, beaches, sights, and bars in the ABC Islands and most of the rest of the southern Caribbean. In their sexy halter or strapless topped mini-skirted sundresses, colored with fuchsia or orange tropical flowers and colorful birds, they prowled the open-air restaurants and bars of the islands. They allowed themselves to be picked up by men looking for a good time and whose pockets were deep, but they always declined to accompany them outside the safety of the bar. Each, having had her fill of marriage, was uninterested in a man at this point. They far preferred the company of each other to that of someone they had to include in every aspect of their lives, from whom they could have no secrets, and who expected of them things they might not want to give. So they went back together to their cruise ship and slept soundly each night.

They also cruised the Mediterranean, and in places like Santorini in Greece and the Amalfi Coast in Italy, they donned their strappy sandals and white Marilyn Monroe sundresses with full skirts and toured the unbelievably rich treasure trove of history they found there, along with the notoriously handsome and romantic swarthy-skinned Mediterranean men. While flirting outrageously with a striped-shirted gondolier in one of the canals in Venice, it happened a time or two that the three capsized their gondola, with gondolier, Annette, Gloria, and Jenny all laughing uproariously while trying to right the boat so they could climb back in. Once the merriment had subsided, the gondolier wasn't quite so happy with his fares, since everything in the boat was now in the bottom of the canal.

Yes, the three friends had an amazing time together. Almost every get-together was an adventure marked by some degree of craziness, daring and skill. Sky diving while bargaining with God to please let the chute open. Deep Sea free-diving where they amazed the scuba divers with their abilities to hang with them without air tanks for a full three minutes. Scuba diving with dolphins and the occasional shark, hoping not to encounter a great white. Spelunking in dripping caverns and caves where they emerge wet and filthy. Crawling on their stomachs in the tight confines of cave tunnels, deep in prayer to not get stuck. Snow-mobiling and speeding on rough, uncharted trails through the pines, dodging trees left and right. Snow skiing on treacherous slopes that slid down to nothingness, sweating in fear under their ski suits. Water skiing in alligator infested waters, exhilarated and hoping not to hit a submerged tree trunk and fly through the air, cartwheeling down into a hungry gator's jaws.

These are a few of the three girls' adventures. But the best adventure of all is when they put on their uniforms of black, mid-calf Capri pants, tight black T-shirts and their lightweight pink athletic-type starter jackets with "The Pink Ladies" in black cursive letters emblazoned on the backs. For that is when Annette *becomes* Sandy, when Gloria becomes Rizzo, and Jenny becomes Frenchy. That's when they truly become who they are. They get into Annette's prized 1958 pink Cadillac convertible with the missile tail lights, they set the boom box to extra loud, and play the soundtrack music from "Grease" while they drive along main street on the Friday afternoon before each football or basketball game, throwing candies, fruit, and small gifts to the underprivileged kids who line the roadside every week waiting for them. If Gloria/Rizzo should sit on the hood of the slow crawling car, and if Jenny/Frenchy should sit on the back over the trunk, and if each should shimmy and shake to the point of almost falling off, well that just adds to the fun. If Annette/Sandy should sing along at the top of her lungs, so loudly that she's horribly out of tune, no one minds. Not even Danny and Sandy could find fault with The Pink Ladies on these Friday afternoons.

They return to Annette's with happiness etched on their countenances. With care, they remove their Pink Lady jackets and hang them carefully in Annette's closet where they reside until they're next called for. They fill fine-stemmed glasses with a good cold, crisp Pinot Grigio or Chardonnay and get out the notepad and pen. They sip their wine and plan their next adventure. The Pink Ladies are now in session.